D1562970

# THE BOY WHO LIVED IN THE CEILING

## CARA THURLBOURN

 WISE WOLF BOOKS  LAS VEGAS

WISE WOLF
BOOKS

This is a work of fiction. All of the characters, organizations, pub-
lications, and events portrayed in this novel are either products of
the author's imagination or are used fictitiously.

THE BOY WHO LIVED IN THE CEILING
Text Copyright © 2021 (As Revised) by Cara Thurlbourn
All rights reserved.

For information, address Wise Wolf Books,
5130 S. Fort Apache Road 215-380 Las Vegas, NV 89148

wisewolfbooks.com

Cover design by Cara Thurlbourn / Wise Wolf Books

ISBN 978-1-953944-08-5 (paperback)
978-1-953944-54-2 (ebook)
LCCN 2021933975

# THE BOY WHO LIVED IN THE CEILING

## AN ANHURST NOVEL

For Grandma Doris

# OCTOBER

OCTOBER

# 1
## FREDDIE

When Freddie reached the crossroads, he turned down Walnut Avenue because it was the long way around. He guessed it was now about one-thirty in the morning. It would be at least three by the time he reached the outskirts of town, which meant he could sit in the all-night café near the taxi stand until the sun came up. If it was quiet, and if Rochelle was there, he might even be able to catch a few minutes' sleep.

Walking slowly, hands in his pockets, he rubbed his thumb over his last two-pound coin, wondering whether he should purchase a coffee to warm his insides or a doughnut because he enjoyed licking the sugary crystals off his lips. He was still undecided and had stopped to scratch his right calf with the toe of his left foot when something caught his attention.

Ahead, about two houses from where he was stand-

ing, a man was sitting in the driver's seat of a silver Ford
Focus, furiously trying to demist the front windshield.
The car was parked in front of a cream bungalow, and
as the man leaned forward, the interior light shone di-
rectly onto the top of his head, illuminating a thinning
patch of hair.

After successfully mopping the windshield with the
sleeve of his navy jacket, the man looked at his watch,
frowned, and stepped out of the car. Again, he examined
his watch, taking a slow, deliberate breath and rubbing
his temples with his forefingers. "That's it," he announced
loudly, striding toward the bungalow. "Time's up."

A short wooden gate separated the man's front garden from the pavement, and it gave a high-pitched creak
as he swung it open, calling, "Ellie, for God's sake hurry
up! We're going to miss the flight!"

"Have you got all the cases?" a woman answered
from somewhere inside.

"All the big ones are in. Seriously, El—we need to go."

"Okay!" the voice replied.

The man hovered at the gate, as if he were unsure
whether to go and help or return to the car. He was still
hovering when a tall, strawberry-haired woman tumbled
out of the front door, a tan handbag slung across her
middle and a small boy gripping the hem of her coat. The
boy was pulling a miniature ladybug-shaped suitcase.

"Pete? Give me a hand?" the woman asked, widening her eyes. Pete took the boy's mittened hand and
grabbed the ladybug, frowning. His wife—Freddie assumed she was his wife—shrugged. "He fell in love with
it; I couldn't say no."

Pete positioned the ladybug in the middle of the back

seat, and the boy climbed in next to it.

"All buckled up, pal?" Pete asked.

The boy nodded.

"Good job."

Freddie stepped closer, careful to stay in the shadow of the neighbor's laurel hedge, and watched the man, Pete, buckle himself into the driver's seat and drum his fingers on the steering wheel. The Focus's doors were still open, and Pete's voice echoed down the street. "I swear to God, if she isn't out here in thirty seconds, we're leaving without her."

"Just give her a minute; she couldn't find her headphones," Ellie replied. "Have you done the GPS?"

"We'll just have to do without."

"After last time?"

"I know where we're going."

Pete started the engine, pulled his door closed, and began to maneuver the car into the road. He stopped when a girl with pale hair and torn jeans emerged from inside the bungalow. Pete beckoned frantically out of the rolled-down car window. The girl raised her index finger indicating "one second" and swung her backpack to the ground. She started pulling things out of it, moving them around and shoving them back in. Pete bit his lower lip as if he were contemplating driving off without her. Eventually, satisfied that whatever she was looking for was safely in the bag, the girl flicked off the hall light, pulled the front door closed, and squeezed in next to her brother and his ladybug.

"Passports and tickets?" Pete asked his wife.

"Yep. All here." She patted her bag, smiling.

"Right, good." Pete exhaled, slowly, as if he were

reminding himself that they were going on vacation and vacations were supposed to be enjoyable. He lightened his tone, tried to make it more singsong, like Ellie's. "Okay, let's go!"

Ellie squeezed Pete's shoulder and lightly kissed his cheek. The blond boy grinned and bunched his fists together, jiggling in his seat. The girl plugged her earbuds into her ears and closed her eyes.

From his hiding place, Freddie watched the family drive away. A memory tugged at his chest, but he ignored it. He decided he would go for the doughnut.

He walked a few paces farther, but when he reached the little wooden gate, he paused to look at the cream bungalow. The front door was painted fire-engine red, and the welcome mat said *Home Sweet Home* in twirly writing. Freddie folded his arms, tucked his hands into the warm grooves of his armpits, and carried on walking.

He had only just reached the next lamppost when a tapping sound broke his concentration. He turned. He waited. There it was again: two taps in quick succession. Freddie walked back to the bungalow. The gate was latched shut. There was no one in sight. He shook his head—he must have been imagining things—and took one last look at the red door.

Oh.

The upper half of a large spiral-bound notebook was wedged in the dark crease of the doorframe—preventing the door from closing.

An icy wind whipped past Freddie's ears.

The door swung in and out, tap-tapping against the book's spine.

Freddie glanced down the avenue. There was nothing—no traffic, no people, no Ford Focus speeding back so Pete and Ellie could check everything was locked up tight.

No one was watching. It would only take a second.

Remembering the creak, Freddie levered himself over the top of the gate and approached the door. He stooped down and nudged it with his elbow to stop it from closing, then placed his fingers on the cool, glossy cover of the notebook.

No one was watching.

# 2
## VIOLET

Violet Johnson did not want to go skiing. She had told her mum they should swap the prize for cash, but her mum had said they'd end up frittering it away and it had been too long, and it would be wonderful. Her dad had agreed with her mum because he always did, and Jamie had been so excited by the idea of snow that he had gone to bed three nights in a row in his scarf and mittens. So, Violet had been outvoted.

On their return, Violet would be starting at Arnhurst, a nearby school with a pretty sketchy reputation. Midway through the fall semester wasn't ideal, but there was no other option. Since being let go, her dad had gone freelance, and there simply weren't enough funds for her and Jamie to both continue in private education. Jamie needed it more than she did, so Violet told her parents that she'd never much liked Briar Ridge anyway and threw herself into studying Arnhurst's prospectus. Their art facilities looked good, which relaxed the creases in her mum's forehead a little. But Violet knew it wasn't going to be easy. She had been practicing not sounding posh. It was a bad habit she'd picked up and she didn't always know she was doing it, but she knew it could be her undoing at Arnhurst.

Jamie's tiny elbow in her ribs jolted her back to the plane cabin. He was frowning and holding out a gray remote with far too many buttons. He wiggled it at her. "What is it, Jay?" she asked. A pointless question, but worth a try.

Jamie wiggled it again, and Violet caught their mum watching them.

"Come on," Violet coaxed, "what do you need?"

On the other side of Jamie, her mum tutted loudly. "Violet, don't be difficult; you can see what he wants." She turned to Jamie and ruffled his hair. "You want me to help you find something, sweetie?"

Violet tried to intervene. "I was just trying to—"

But their mum's attention was now firmly on Jamie, scrutinizing his face as she scrolled through the kids' channels until his eyes lit up. "This one?"

Jamie nodded, and their mum pressed play.

From across the aisle, their dad reached over and tugged Violet's sleeve. "Dr. What's-Her-Face says we mustn't push him, love; you know that. He'll speak when he's ready."

Violet sighed and jammed her headphones back in. Dr. What's-Her-Face was a moron.

# 3
## FREDDIE

The front door clicked shut, and Freddie leaned against it, clasping the notebook against his chest. He didn't know what had made him step inside. He had intended to tuck the book back through the opening, pull the door shut, and go to the all-night café to buy his doughnut. But the smell trickling out from the hallway had stopped him. It was warmth and Sundays and home-cooked meals. And it called him inside.

Above the dull hum of household electronics, a clock ticked. Crisp fingers of nighttime air seeped through the door behind him. Freddie shivered and stepped a little deeper into the hallway. Somewhere to his right, a blue dot blinked on and off in the darkness. His breath caught in his throat, until he realized it was the thermostat and not a burglar alarm. Gently, he skimmed his fingers along the wall until he came across a radiator, turned down low and cocooned in a force field of warm air. If he just sat down for a minute or two, he could warm up. Prepare himself for the rest of the night.

Resting his back against the radiator's warm grooves, knees folded against his chest, Freddie sighed and sank down a little lower. He stifled a yawn. His eyelids were heavy and thick with sleep. If he just closed them for a minute...

* * *

Six hours later, daylight began to trickle through the frosty glass pane in the red door. A pile of envelopes clattered through the mailbox, landing on the oatmeal carpet with a thud.

Freddie opened his eyes. He blinked. His surroundings were unfamiliar. He tried to remember where he slept last night but found all he could think of was donuts. Beneath his head, the contents of his bag had formed an uncomfortable mound at the base of his skull, and his neck was tight and stiff. He looked up. The ceiling was white and dimpled, the texture of popcorn. He remembered the girl with pale hair and the boy with the ladybug suitcase.

Leaning on the radiator, Freddie stood up. His joints creaked, and his head swayed as if it was too large for his body. He remembered the tapping sound, the open door, and the notebook he was still holding. Then he noticed the pile of envelopes and, instinctively, he scooped them up from the floor and set them neatly on the hall table, noting the surname that appeared on each: Johnson.

Next to the table where Freddie set the mail there was

a pair of double doors with glass panels in their middles. Through the panels, he could see a large black television and the edge of a wooden coffee table. Freddie lingered for a moment. He knew he should leave—scatter the envelopes back on the floor, abandon the notebook in the hall, and close the door behind him. But now that it was daylight outside someone might see him. And if that happened, he would have to explain. What would he say? Who would believe him if he told them it had been an accident? Better to wait until it was dark.

Before going any farther, Freddie removed his shoes and his threadbare socks, ignoring the dirt beneath his toenails. The living room door handles were bright and shiny, so he pulled his sleeves down over his fingers before he touched them.

At the end of the room, a large bay window looked out onto Walnut Avenue, but the curtains were almost all the way closed. Next to the television, an empty fireplace was lined with delicately patterned tiles that Freddie's mum would have liked. In its center, a wooden heart-shaped frame displayed a collage of photographs. Freddie knelt and touched its rim with the tip of his finger. A formal family portrait was positioned proudly in the middle, but the images around the edges were his favorites. There was the blond boy grinning a nearly toothless grin, with ice cream smeared across his cheeks; Mr. Johnson and Mrs. Johnson, peering up at the camera, pouting; the pale-haired girl stretched out on the ground making a snow angel; a birthday cake with candles; a campfire.

Opposite the fireplace was a brown leather sofa covered with tartan throws and mis-matched cushions. Freddie longed to press his palm onto one of the cushions and test its plumpness. But he didn't.

The Johnsons' living room opened into a bright, open-plan kitchen and dining area. On the kitchen worktop, next to the toaster, lay a plate of crumbs and a knife smeared with butter—abandoned. Freddie's stomach lurched into a growl. He tried to calculate when he had last eaten. Yesterday? The day before? Gingerly, he opened the cupboard nearest the kettle, instinct telling him that was where the cups might be kept. He chose a plastic mug decorated with Disney characters and filled it with cloudy tap water. He drank without stopping. Then he rinsed his cup and scrubbed his hands with the green prickly side of the sponge until they felt clean.

His stomach rumbled again, louder this time. Thinking that he might find something nearly out-of-date that no one would miss, he opened the large, black fridge-freezer. Toward the back, wedged behind the butter, he found half a cheese and tomato sandwich (on white bread). It was soggy, and there were a few blue-green specks of mold on the cheese. The Johnsons had probably forgotten it was there.

Freddie forced himself to eat the sandwich slowly, leaning over the kitchen sink to prevent any crumbs dropping to the floor. He had read somewhere that if you pictured the food traveling down to your stomach, *really* concentrated on each mouthful, you remained fuller for longer. He wasn't sure if it worked, but he often did it just in case it made a difference.

On finishing the sandwich, Freddie became urgently aware of the pressure in his bladder. He returned to the hallway. One door was locked, but the second opened into another hall. With relief, he read a small plaque that said *Salle de Bain* and hurriedly entered the bathroom to relieve himself. A glass shelf next to the sink housed an assortment of bottles: hand soap, face wash, body lotion, hand lotion, face lotion. All in different colors and scents. But Freddie settled for the creamy bar of soap that had almost glued itself to the basin and rinsed his hands. Then he bent and splashed warm water on his face.

Looking up, he noticed his reflection. When he had first found himself with nowhere to sleep, he had visited the public restrooms near the bus station every morning to wash his face and put water on his hair so it wasn't so fluffy. But eventually the fluff had morphed into grease and his clothes had started to smell. The weather had turned colder. And the effort of it had become simply too much.

The last time Freddie had studied himself in a mirror, his hair had been a vivid fiery shade of auburn, slightly wavy but cut so it could be tamed with wax or gel. He had never minded being ginger. In fact, he loved it. Especially after *Harry Potter* and the whole Ron Weasley thing. He knew he had unusually green eyes and a strong jaw. He knew girls looked at him as he walked down the street.

In the Johnsons' mirror, however, he did not see Freddie with the strong jaw and the sparkling eyes. He saw sunken cheeks and muted freckles. His chin was covered in thin, incongruous patches of stubble. He wanted to scrub his hands again.

On the edge of the bathtub, he spotted a pink disposable razor. The blades were tinged with rust, but Freddie squeezed some shaving foam into his palm and attacked the fuzz on his chin. Then he removed his jeans, his pants, his coat, the dark red hoodie from the charity reject pile, and his graying vest. He folded his gangly frame into the bath and held the shower hose over his head. The water was cool, and he didn't know how to adjust the temperature, but he remained in the bath until the water ran clear.

Ten minutes later, his neck dotted with tissue, his skin pink and bumpy, Freddie stood, pale and naked, in the hall near the bathroom. He had deposited his clothes in the Johnsons' washing machine and left his last remaining two pounds in a glass jar in the kitchen labelled *Rainy Day Funds*—payment for the water, electric, and shaving foam.

As his clothes whirled round and round, shedding their staleness, Freddie stared at a photograph: a framed print that showed Mr. Johnson in a dark-gray suit, crisp white shirt, and pale-blue tie, shaking hands with a short Japanese man. Freddie shuffled his feet. A pang of embarrassment gnawed at his ribs. He remembered his dad owning a suit like that once, remembered the flush of pride he'd felt as he watched his father's broad-shouldered frame leaving for work. He remembered his dad saying, "One day you'll be needing a suit like this. We'll go together and get you measured up." He remembered his dad patting the crown of his head and tousling his hair. But he might have made that up.

Somewhere in the back of Freddie's mind, a thought began to niggle. He shook his head but, as he examined Mr. Johnson's smooth chin and glossy brown shoes, the niggle grew larger. Perhaps it wasn't a bad idea after all? Freddie felt a grin stretch open his lips. If he borrowed a suit, he could go to the job center. He had been once before, in his long coat and ratty sweater; someone had told him there were zero-hours contracts available with a local pizza delivery firm and that they weren't fussy as long as you had a clean record. But the lady behind the desk had given him such a narrow, withering look that he had simply turned around and walked back out without saying a word. If he borrowed one of Mr. Johnson's suits, he would look older and more distinguished, the way his father used to. They would take him seriously. "A good suit can make a man's fortune," his dad had said.

Freddie padded down the hall. Ellie and Pete's bedroom door was wide open. In the center of the room, cushions and a quilt lay crumpled at the foot of the bed. Opposite the bed, there was a wardrobe with mirrored doors. Freddie concentrated on ignoring his reflection and opened it. The doors creaked briefly and then settled. Most of the space was taken up with an assortment of dresses, skirts, blouses, and scarves, but a small section on the left was reserved for Pete's pants and shirts. Freddie couldn't see the gray suit from the photograph but picked out a smart black pair of pants, a matching jacket, a white shirt with thin blue pinstripes, and a blue tie. From the bottom of the wardrobe, he took a pair of black leather shoes. The pants were a little short and the shoes a little big, but when Freddie saw himself in the Johnsons' bedroom mirror, he knew his plan would work.

\* \* \*

He found the key for the back door hanging on a hook in the utility and let himself out into the garden. He was hoping to find a side gate that he could sneak through but discovered that all the properties on Walnut Avenue were connected by a public footpath that ran along the back of their gardens. Listening first, in case anyone was passing by, Freddie slipped out of the Johnsons' dark green gate and, feet sliding inside Pete Johnson's shiny black shoes, made his way to the town center.

As he approached the job center, Freddie squared his shoulders, lifted his chin, and brushed his shirt.

He pushed the door. It didn't open. He pulled. It still didn't open. Someone walked up beside him; a woman. "They're closed. Took me hours to get here on the bus." She looked tired, and her hair was scraped back into a tight ponytail, giving her a surprised expression that didn't match the tone of her voice.

"Do you know how long for?"

"Doesn't say." The woman tapped the door, pointing out a handwritten sign:

*CLOSED DUE TO FLOODING.*
*If you have an appointment or your enquiry is urgent please call 07844212056.*
*We will do our best to open as soon as possible.*

"Helpful," Freddie muttered.

The woman shrugged and walked away.

Freddie's cheeks reddened. He felt foolish. Without a contact address or telephone number, the job center wouldn't have been able to help him anyway—suit or no suit. Perhaps the flood was a blessing.

Hands in his pockets, trying to ignore the tight twang of anxiousness that was prickling his chest, Freddie trudged back along the main street. He paused outside Starbucks and wished he hadn't left his two pounds in the rainy-day jar. He fished into Pete's jacket, hoping to find some coins that he could repay later. Nothing.

"Excuse me, are you okay?" Someone was lightly tapping his arm.

Freddie turned, muscles tense.

"Are you okay?" the man repeated himself. He didn't look much older than Freddie, maybe in his early twenties. He had floppy brown hair and was wearing a checked scarf wound tightly around his neck.

"Forgot my wallet." Freddie shrugged, trying to sound truthful.

"Oh, what rotten luck," the man replied.

"I'll have to make do with the vending machine back at the office." Freddie rolled his eyes, slipping into character and imitating the man's upper-class lilt.

The floppy-haired man grimaced. "Gosh, well we can't have that!" he laughed. "Here, take this."

Freddie's eyes widened as the stranger shoved a crisp five-pound note into his hand.

"Oh, no, I couldn't..." He tried to hand it back.

"I insist," the man replied, already walking away. "Enjoy!"

* * *

Freddie leaned back against the coffee shop window and slid the note into his pocket. He remembered the first time he'd been given money by a stranger. Like so many other significant moments in his life, it had been unplanned—an accident.

It was the day the repossession agents had come, with their clipboards and sheets of paper. Freddie had expected them to be cruel, had anticipated them making jokes and his dad blowing up, starting a fight, the police being called. Instead, the older man with dimples in his cheeks had patted his dad's arm and made them cups of tea while his colleague went through the paperwork, taking signatures and explaining.

Despite being sympathetic, after the paperwork they removed the TV and Freddie's Xbox—the car had gone months ago—and then there wasn't much left, so Freddie's dad told them to pack their bags, they were leaving. They could have waited for a letter from the council, but his dad said he knew what it would say and there was no point.

A few hours later, they piled into a car they'd borrowed from their next-door neighbor's son and drove toward the park, boxes and plastic bags jammed all the way to the roof. Freddie's dad stopped the car and took a flask from his jacket pocket. In the front passenger seat, Janet stared straight ahead, her hands braced on the dashboard, her fingertips whitening with the pressure. Freddie put his hand on her shoulder, and she flinched as though her skin were burning.

Freddie's dad looked at his wife, then at his son, and took another swig of whiskey.

"Dad, do you want me to drive?" Freddie asked, the words escaping his lips before he had chance to stop them.

For a moment, there was silence. Then, his father flung open the driver's door and made a sound that was almost a roar. "Get out," he bellowed, pulling the back passenger door open and grappling for Freddie's collar. Freddie tried to scramble backward, but the boxes and bags were rammed up against him and he couldn't escape. His father's hands were around his throat. Janet was not moving.

"Dad, I'm sorry..." Freddie pleaded between gasps.

The hands loosened and Freddie thought it was over, but then they were taking hold of his ankles and pulling, dragging him out of the car. "I said get out!"

Freddie was sprawled on the pavement, his arms up around his ears, anticipating a kick. His father reached back into the car and tossed his backpack at his feet. "Take your shit and leave. I don't want to see you again," he spat.

The car screeched as it accelerated into the distance. Freddie had no idea where they were going. Janet had said something about calling her mother, but Freddie didn't know Janet's mother's name or address. At first, he thought it had started to rain, but then he realized his face was wet because he was crying.

He stayed on the pavement, half propped up on his elbows, bag at his feet, waiting for his dad to come back. Surely, Janet would tell him to come back. Surely, they wouldn't leave him. He tried calling his dad's cell phone, but there was no answer. He texted saying sorry and asking them to call. But he couldn't remember whether the phone had been given to the repo agents or not.

In his wallet, he counted two pounds and fifty-seven pence. His debit card was useless; he had handed over the last of his savings months ago. So, Freddie slung his bag over his shoulder and walked toward the town center. He ignored Starbucks, Costa, Café Nero and headed for the gray greasy spoon at the end of the main street.

The coffee he ordered was thick and sour, but he drank it anyway. And, as he drank, he realized he had nowhere to go. They were new to the area, and he'd been due to start school that September. He thought of contacting his friends from back home but couldn't bear the thought of explaining what had happened since he left. Besides, his dad and Janet would probably come looking for him, so he'd better not stray too far.

The café closed at six p.m. Freddie had been fiddling with his empty coffee cup for two hours. He thought the waitress might ask him to leave or order another drink, but she seemed neither to notice or care—content with perching on a stool behind the counter, reading a magazine and re-glossing her lips. Finally, though, she began to mop the floor and stack the chairs and Freddie said goodnight.

Stepping onto the dark pavement, he shivered violently. The sun had given way to a foggy night sky, and dampness clung to his skin. Freddie pulled his coat a little tighter and turned back toward the park. When he reached the memorial at the end of the main street, he stopped and perched on its bottom step. He removed his woolly hat, the one Amy had gotten him for Christmas, and he'd pretended to hate, placed it on his lap, and pushed his fingers through his hair.

"Here you go, mate," mumbled a low voice, swooping quickly past. Freddie looked down: a two-pound coin. A few minutes later, from a lady with a red scarf, some copper coins and a fifty pence piece joined the two pounds.

By seven thirty, rush hour was over, and the hum of traffic had reduced to a whisper. Freddie had collected four pounds and eighty-nine pence. Gratitude and embarrassment swelled in his stomach.

\* \* \*

Now, leaning against Starbucks window, Freddie wrapped his arms around himself, talons of memory gripping his shoulders and making him wince. The money he'd made that first day had been generous. In the eighteen months since, he'd been lucky to average three pounds and some empty candy wrappers each day.

Freddie couldn't understand what made today different, why the man with the scarf had been so generous. He looked down at his shoes, wondering how Mr. Johnson kept them so untarnished. He thought of his own shoes, dirty and worn. He stroked his stubble-free chin...

His clothes were different. But it couldn't be because of his clothes. Could it? Surely, people wouldn't give *more* money to someone who looked as if they needed it *less*?

He waited a few minutes, and then when a middle-aged man in a long brown coat walked toward him, he said, "Excuse me, I'm so sorry to bother you, I'm so embarrassed..."

The man stopped and frowned. Freddie's nerves jangled, but he pressed on. "I forgot my wallet, and my boss asked me to get him a coffee. It's my first day. I don't suppose I could trouble you..." He trailed off. He didn't know where the lie came from and was surprised he found it so easy.

The man's expression softened, and he chuckled. "Of course! Can't have you getting fired on your first day, can we, son?"

Freddie followed him inside, and the man, whose name was Charles, bought Freddie's fictitious boss a large cappuccino and a blueberry muffin. Freddie thanked him profusely, but Charles merely shrugged. "No problem. It's the company card anyway."

To make absolutely certain it wasn't a fluke, Freddie spent the rest of the day moving from shop to shop, telling variations on the theme of lost wallets, angry bosses, and forgotten bus passes. All in all, he was given nineteen pounds, in a combination of notes and coins, a sandwich, a Diet Coke, the cappuccino, the blueberry muffin and, finally, a bus ticket back to Walnut Avenue.

Maybe his father had been right after all. Maybe a suit really could make a man's fortune.

# 4
# FREDDIE

Back at the Johnsons', having let himself in through the garden gate, Freddie counted his wares: nineteen pounds and a day's worth of food. He laid the notes next to one another on the kitchen table. Then he stacked the coins. Nineteen pounds. If he did this every day for a week, he'd collect one hundred and thirty-three pounds. That's over five hundred a month...

Freddie's brain was whirring; he could rent a room, find a job, go to school.

He pushed back his chair, and it screeched against the tiled floor. Ridiculous. After a couple of days, the suit would be crumpled and dirty, and he'd be back to square one. Unless... No, it was impossible; he couldn't. He was pacing now, up and down. Unless he could stay in the bungalow...

Freddie sat back down, rested his head in his hands,

and told himself to think logically. He glanced up at the calendar on the fridge. Today was October the second. Three weeks were blocked out in black marker pen with *VACATION!!!* scrawled above them and smiley faces drawn around the edges. Three weeks.

His stomach tightened, and his skin prickled. Surely this could never work? Someone would find out. He would be arrested. But then, what did he have to lose?

Freddie needed the internet. Three weeks in the Johnsons' home, wearing a suit and collecting money, would allow him to save around three hundred pounds—if today was a fair example of what to expect. But there was no point even contemplating it until he knew whether he could use the money to make some kind of difference to his situation. So, making sure the curtains were pulled as tightly shut as possible, he turned on the TV and navigated clumsily to the browser. The remote was heavy and had lots of buttons. He used to be quicker at these things.

On findaroom.uk he typed in the Johnsons' postcode, then sorted the results so they appeared lowest price first. There were heaps of them—rooms in shared houses—starting at one-fifty a month. He looked through at least fifteen, checking the deposit amount and whether the first month's rent was due in advance. Of those, ten asked for deposits of less than two-hundred, and seven asked for nothing up front. They required a reference, but he was sure someone from the shelter could help him with that; they knew him well enough.

Two months. Three hundred pounds would buy him two months in his own room, with space to breathe and think and be himself again. And he was sure to find at least a zero-hours contract in that time. He just needed the money to start things off.

* * *

An hour later, Freddie had formed a plan: He would camp out at the Johnsons' until they returned from their vacation. He would invest his initial earnings and purchase some smart clothing from the charity shop. Nineteen pounds should be enough.

By now, his own clothes were dry, and he put them back on despondently. There wasn't enough time to make it back into town before the shops closed, so Freddie took his donated sandwich and crouched on the living room floor opposite the television. He picked up the remote, wondering what was on now at this time of day. He pointed it at the screen, then lowered it. Mustn't get too comfortable.

Creamy sandwich filling dribbled onto Freddie's chin. He ate quickly this time and licked the wrapper when he was finished. His mum would have tutted at that. "You don't know where it's been," she would have said, rolling her eyes and letting him do it anyway.

Outside, the sky had darkened, and the streetlights of Walnut Avenue were flickering to life. An orange glow illuminated the Johnsons' living room. Freddie stretched out on the rug in front of the unlit fire. He closed his eyes. "Think warm thoughts," his mum had always said when Freddie complained that his bedroom was cold. "Imagine you're nice and toasty and warm, and you'll soon feel better."

The next morning, Freddie drank a glass of nearly sour milk and, this time, took the bus into town. The charity shop run by the local hospice was at the end of a side street near the memorial. A bell jingled as he pushed open the door. Madge, who worked in the shop three mornings a week, was rearranging a shelf of children's books. Madge was seventy; he knew this because he'd seen her husband arrive with a balloon and a large bunch of flowers on her birthday. Freddie often walked past the shop on the days Madge worked because she had a kind smile and twinkly blue eyes. It was Madge who had given him the red hoodie.

He tapped her on the shoulder and said, "Hi."

Madge turned and slid her glasses to the end of her nose. "Can I help you?" she asked.

"It's..." He was about to say, *It's me, Freddie,* when she interrupted him.

"Freddie?" She was examining his clean-shaven chin.

"Yes. Uh. Hi," he stuttered. "I'm looking for a suit."

"A suit?" Madge smiled. "Well, that's an unusual request." She set down her pile of books. "Let's see what we've got."

On a rack toward the back of the shop was an assortment of pants and shirts. "Welcome to the menswear section," Madge winked as she started to sift through the clothes.

She pulled out several pairs of pants and some smart, long-sleeved shirts but couldn't find a matching jacket. "Hang on," she said, "let me check out the back. We had some bags delivered yesterday."

Freddie examined the shirts: four pounds each. The pants were six. That only left nine.

Madge returned brandishing a wide grin. "I think you're in luck!" she said, presenting Freddie with a black plastic suit-carrier. "Have a look."

He unzipped the bag. Inside was a spotless gray suit. "Why would someone throw this away?"

Madge shrugged, "People get bored of things, I suppose. Do you want to try it on?"

Freddie said yes, please, and Madge ushered him into a tiny, curtained cubicle at the back of the shop. The pants were a little baggy, but the jacket was a perfect fit; he had broad shoulders like his father.

Madge clapped her hands when he drew back the curtain, "Marvelous!" she said. "Just the ticket. But you need a shirt too."

"I'm not sure I have enough. How much is the suit?"

Madge tapped the edge of her lip with her little finger. "How much do you have?"

Freddie handed over his notes and coins. "Oh, well I should think this will do," she said. "And I should imagine it'll be enough for a pair of shoes as well."

"Thank you," he said.

Madge squeezed his arm. "Don't thank me, dear, just make sure you get the job."

"Job?"

"The suit? It's for an interview isn't it?"

"Oh... yes. An interview." A pang of guilt nudged his stomach. When had lying become so easy?

Half an hour later, after changing in his old restrooms near the bus station, Freddie lingered near the café at the top of the town. The first person he asked scowled and said, "Nah, mate." The second tutted. Perhaps he had made a mistake. Perhaps yesterday was a fluke. He wondered whether Madge would take the suit back.

And then it worked, just like that. "Sure," said a woman in a cream coat. "I don't have any change but take this..." She had handed him a ten-pound note.

# 5

## VIOLET

Violet was alone in the hotel room. Her mum and dad were trying out one of the super-scary, adult-only slopes, and Jamie was at some kind of craft-making kids' club. After a solid week of quality time with her family it was nice to wallow in solitude for a bit.

Alone with her iPhone and a Wi-Fi connection, Violet finally allowed herself to check her email. She'd been resisting it ever since they left home. Partly because her mum had insisted they have a tech-free vacation (Violet suspected this was more aimed at her dad than at herself). But also, because she was afraid contact with the outside world would cause her to start missing her friends.

Violet didn't do "social-media". Her best friend, Aisla, had read a book about the detrimental effects it can have on self-esteem, cognitive ability, all sorts, and so—along with a couple of other hangers-on—they had decided to remove themselves from the fray and go old school. Violet, Aisla, Daisy, and Pati communicated via email and text only.

She had expected her inbox to be brimming with emails from Aisla and the girls; group conversations about things she already felt left out of. But, instead, there were just three:

From: **Aisla Buchanan**
Subject: **Miss you already, boo**

*Can't believe you're really gone. Life sucks without you. Hope the skiing is fabulous. Take pics of hot chalet boys. Love you.*

From: **Aisla Buchanan**
Subject: **Florida**

*You will never believe this: Daisy's mum's taking us to Florida over the school break! All three of us! You'd have been invited too, obvs, but you're off on your fancy-pants ski trip. We're staying in this amazing Airbnb place. Pool, games room, probs even a private chef. I'll send pics. Love you.*

From: **Aisla Buchanan**
Cc: **Daisy London, Pati Reed**
Subject: **Discommunicating**

*Okay, so we're in Florida and it's amazing. Daisy's mum introduced us to this incredible yoga teacher called Toto. She's a bit of a hippy, but she's so in tune with her spirit. She's got tons of books on connecting with nature and relinquishing modern lifestyles that*

*make us stressed and damage our health. The stuff
she says just makes so much sense. Honestly, Vi, you
would LOVE her.*

*Toto says that technology and consumer-driven nar-
cissistic social media practices are basically like the
work of the devil—well, not the actual devil, but you
know what I mean. Anyway, me, Daisy, and Patts, we've
decided we're going to stop all email and text communication—apart from emergencies. And no more internet
either, except for doing homework. Toto says it's like
detoxing from modern life.*

*So, when you're back, call our landlines—our phones
will probably be switched off.*

*Love and peace.*

Violet read Aisla's final email three times and cringed.
Had she sounded this childish and sanctimonious
when she'd lectured her mum about her decision to
quit Facebook? She looked down at her phone and
scrolled through her contacts; she didn't even have
their landlines.

Violet sighed. She'd expected it to take a couple of
months, at least, for their friendship to fade away, but it
had started already; this sudden move toward communication via carrier pigeon had cemented Violet's place
as an outsider. No one at the new school would even
contemplate socializing with her if she started talking
about *consumer-driven narcissistic social media practices*—whatever that even meant. But if she didn't go
along with it, Aisla would cast her out. Perhaps Aisla had
already cast her out and this was just a not-so-gentle
way of cutting ties.

Violet flopped back onto the bed and buried her head in her pillow. A tap on the door forced her to come up for air. She shoved her phone back into her bedside drawer and straightened the pillow. "One second," she called.

When she opened the door, she was greeted by a frowning brunette who looked only a little older than Violet herself. "I'm sorry, he got very agitated," said the brunette.

Something tugged at Violet's leg, and she looked down to see Jamie pushing past her, scurrying into the room and heading straight for the wardrobe. "Oh," said Violet.

The brunette shook her head. "So sorry." Her name tag read *Hi, I'm Krystal, Kids' Play Worker at The Bromley Hotel.*

"What did you do to upset him?" Violet asked, noticing the venom in her tone but not attempting to quash it.

Krystal shifted nervously from foot to foot. "We were all introducing ourselves, playing the clap game? You know," she clapped her hands twice and her face morphed into an overexcited smile, "Krystal!"

Violet folded her arms.

Krystal cleared her throat. "We were trying to encourage Jamie to join in, but..." She glanced toward the wardrobe. "Well, he got very upset and hid under the table. It took us ages to get him out. We tried calling your parents, but—"

"They're up on the slope."

Krystal made an "ah" shape with her mouth but didn't speak.

Violet lowered her voice and pulled the door a little behind her. "Didn't Mum explain about his talking?

Didn't they tell you?"

"Well, ah, maybe my manager?" Krystal was stuttering now. "I wasn't supposed to be on shift, they called me last minute—"

"Right, well, I expect my parents will be wanting a word with your manager when they get back."

Krystal nodded and backed away, toward the elevator. Violet stepped back into the room and shut the door, leaning against it for a moment, looking up at the ceiling and trying not to cry. She was picturing Jamie's little cheeks growing redder and his heart hammering in his chest as that ridiculous woman clapped and clapped and tried to force him to talk in front of everyone. His worst nightmare.

She took a deep breath and headed over to the wardrobe. "Jay," she whispered. "You okay, little man?" Of course, there was no answer.

"Wait there," said Violet. She left Jamie in the wardrobe and went to the mini fridge, retrieved the two ginormous Snickers bars that their dad had explicitly warned them not to touch because they were six pounds apiece, and a can of Diet Coke. Then, she opened the wardrobe doors and clambered inside. Jamie was crouched behind the complimentary robes with his knees tucked up and his forehead down. Violet wriggled in beside him and pulled the doors closed behind her. "Snickers?" she asked.

Violet couldn't see Jamie's face, but she knew he'd be looking at her quizzically. "Dad won't mind," she said. "If he does, I'll give him the money. I've not spent any of my allowance yet." Jamie's tiny fingers reached out and took the chocolate bar. She heard him deftly opening the wrapper and beginning to nibble. She opened the Diet Coke. The snap and fizz always made Jamie smile. "Beverage, sir?" she asked in a posh voice. Jamie took the drink and slurped loudly, then handed it back to Violet and rested his head on her arm.

They stayed in the wardrobe, eating their forbidden chocolate bars and sipping Diet Coke until their mum returned. Violet guessed it had been at least an hour because her backside was beginning to feel numb against the hard wooden floor. She and Jamie were experts at making chocolate last an inordinately long time. It was a rare treat at home, so they savored every mouthful.

"Vi?" their mum called. Her voice was singsong and a little out of puff. "Violet?"

Violet pushed open the wardrobe door and straightened out her legs, gesturing behind her. "Jamie's in there."

Their mum frowned. "I thought he was still at the craft thing? Dad's gone to pick him up."

Just as their mum finished speaking, the bedroom door flew open and their dad whirled in, his cheeks a violent shade of red. "That woman!" he shouted. "Where is he? Where's Jamie?"

"Vi says he's in the wardrobe," their mum answered. "What's going on, Pete?"

Their dad was pulling off his jacket and boots. "Bloody woman—tried to make him introduce himself to everyone, something about clapping? No idea, but she said he freaked out and hid under the table. Didn't you tell her about his problems?" He pronounced *problems* as though it was the name of a terrible disease.

"Of course, I did; I told the manager—Diane Something-or-Other."

"Well Diane Something-or-Other wasn't there, just some teenager with no brain cells."

Violet stepped in between her parents and pointed toward the wardrobe, dropping her voice to a whisper. "Maybe you should have this conversation later? He's already upset."

Her mum shot her dad a sideways glance, then hurried over to the wardrobe. "Jamie, sweetheart, we're not angry with you. Mummy and Daddy were just upset that you had a bad time of it. That's all. It wasn't your fault..."

Her mum talked at the wardrobe for half an hour with no success. She even tried crawling inside, like Violet had, but Jamie stomped his feet and waved his arms, and she gave up. Eventually, Violet suggested room-service pizza, and when it arrived hunger tempted Jamie back into the room. He emerged clutching his Snickers wrapper, his eyes pinched against the brightness. Their dad eyed the wrapper but didn't say anything. Neither did Jamie. As always, he was silent. He simply hopped up onto the bed and handed Violet the remote. "Movie?" she asked. He nodded.

Violet flicked through the children's films until Jamie squeezed her hand. He had chosen *Finding Nemo*, one of Violet's favorites. Jamie snuggled up close to his sister, and Violet wrapped her arm around him. Their mum and dad spread out the pizza boxes at the end of the bed and handed them each a napkin. Then they all sat eating pizza, watching the film, and not talking, together.

# 6

## FREDDIE

Freddie had been living in the Johnsons' home for ten days when he finally ventured into the room belonging to the pale-haired girl. Until then, he had limited himself to the living room, the bathroom, and the kitchen. For the first three days, he hadn't even allowed himself to sit on the sofa. He had left each morning as soon as the going-to-work traffic died down and returned late. In the evenings, after letting himself back in and returning the key to the thingamabobs tin, he would sit at the dining table and count his donations, eating whatever food he'd been given by the people who assumed he was an honest, young working professional without a wallet. He was astounded that his plan continued to work. He kept waiting for someone to realize he was faking it, but no one did. He didn't mind so much when the ones with designer shoes and wallets that smelled of real leather gave him money. But when the stooped ladies with gray hair and thick cardigans squeezed his forearm, said, "Of course, dear," and gave him a pound coin, his throat constricted so much he could barely manage to say thank you.

He'd kept everything tidy, determined to leave no trace of himself. If he used a plate, he washed it and put it straight back in the cupboard. If he took a shower, he mopped up the wet footprints and hung his towel neatly back on the rack. He drank tap water and bought a box of generic cornflakes and some long-life milk to eat in the mornings. And every few days, when he washed his clothes, he slipped a pound into the rainy-day jar because he felt guilty about using the water and electric.

The thing that bothered him most was leaving the plate with crumbs and the buttery knife sitting on the worktop. He longed to rinse them and put them back where they belonged, but he couldn't because someone might ask, "Who washed the plate?" and then start to notice other things—a cushion out of place, the missing cheese sandwich—and call the police, who would dust for fingerprints. A neighbor might say they had seen him "lingering and looking suspicious" the night the Johnsons went away. They might provide a description, do an E-FIT likeness of Freddie. His dad might see it on TV—his son, the intruder. So, Freddie left the plate where it was.

The Johnsons' home did not remind him of his own: it was softer and warmer. Warmth was something Janet had struggled with. She liked things to be neat and straight. She enjoyed muted shades of beige and gray and had installed a sleek, glossy kitchen that looked like something from a catalogue. He often wondered why his father had chosen to marry someone so very different from his mother.

Freddie's mother would have liked the Johnsons' house; she was the kind of person who bought cushions and throws, hung posters in frames and painted old pieces of furniture instead of buying new ones. When he pictured her, she was always *doing*. Even when they sat watching television in the evenings, waiting for his dad to return from the office, she would be knitting or sewing or gluing pieces of broken tiles to the top of a shabby old coffee table. In those days, his father never complained about the mess. Instead, he would kiss his wife's forehead and say, "You clever old thing," and she would smile as though he was the sun and the moon and everything in between.

Freddie liked remembering them like that. His mother had brought out the best in his father. After she'd gone, his father had gathered every object that reflected a fragment of who she was and locked it away in the attic until, two years later, Janet had listed it all on eBay and got rid of it all.

* * *

It was the notebook that led him to the girl's room. Freddie had forgotten all about it, but on the tenth day he happened to glance in its direction as he returned from the bathroom. He assumed it was hers because she was the last to leave the house and had been puttering with her bag on the doorstep. He thought he should probably return it to her room, so it looked like she'd forgotten it.

The room next to the bathroom belonged to the small

boy, full of bright colors and stuffed toys. Freddie closed his eyes and pulled the door shut, his throat tightening as he remembered Amy and her princess room. It hadn't been very Janet-like, but eventually, after months of "Pleeeaase, Mummy," his stepmother had caved and purchased a bright pink bed with a floating canopy and twinkling fairy lights. Amy had loved it so much she'd made Freddie camp out with her for two whole nights.

He breathed deeply, in through his nose and out through his mouth, exhaling the memory away.

Opposite the bathroom was the girl's bedroom. He had expected grungy teenage posters, an unmade bed, and piles of unwashed clothes. But what he found was anything but grungy. The first thing he noticed was the curtains. They weren't really curtains but wide strips of multi-colored fabric hanging from a bronze pole. Between the strips, he could see that they didn't obscure a window but a glass door that opened onto a small square courtyard. In the corner of the room there was a desk strewn with pens, pencils, and pieces of charcoal. Above the desk, a host of elaborate pen and ink sketches lined the wall.

Freddie moved closer, transfixed. Each sketch contained a hundred different elements, intricately woven together: trees, birds, rivers, plants, women with flowing hair and delicate features. Each drawing was different, like something from a fairy tale. There were castles and oceans and clouds. Freddie brushed his fingers across the surface of the artwork, convinced they must have been prints taken from a book or a website, but they were real.

He set the notebook on the desk and flipped it open.

The name *Violet* was scrawled across the front page, decorated with doodles of flowers and fairies. The rest of the pages were blank. He closed the book and moved it to the back of the desk, covering it with an untidy pile of thick paper so it looked like she had accidentally missed it when packing. *Violet.* It was a good name.

Next to the desk was a bulletin board crowded with postcards of famous paintings, clippings from newspapers, and old sepia photographs of a lady with neat, dark hair and perfect skin. Violet's bed was covered in an assortment of patchwork blankets and turquoise cushions, but the corner nearest the door was the real surprise; hanging from the ceiling was a wicker egg-shaped chair lined with a deep blue cushion. A book and a pair of glasses had been casually abandoned on the seat. Freddie pictured Violet curled in the chair with her legs tucked beneath her, reading and sketching and wearing cool-girl glasses, and felt instantly out of her league. She was the kind of girl he'd always wanted to be with but never had the guts to pursue. Instead, he'd ended up with the bland ones, the ones with long hair and full lips who jutted out their breasts when they spoke to him because, on some level, they were aware that the things they were saying weren't very interesting.

Freddie was relieved he would never have to brave a conversation with Violet Johnson. Maybe one day, when he'd sorted himself out and had a job, he'd find a girl like her and manage to be charming and funny and convince her to go out with him. But not now. Not like this.

Freddie closed Violet's door and returned to the living room. He glanced at the clock: eight a.m. An hour until his usual departure time. As he had done so many times before over the last fortnight, he picked up the TV remote and held it, weighed it up and down in his hand, ran his fingers over the buttons. Not allowing himself to watch TV had been a way of ensuring he didn't forget that his situation was temporary. But as each day passed and Freddie felt more and more at home in the Johnsons' bungalow, it became harder to resist.

He slapped the remote back down on the coffee table, then shoved it under one of the sofa cushions because perhaps if it was out of sight, he wouldn't be so tempted. He was just about to go and make coffee (he'd bought himself a jar of the stuff Janet used to say was "rancid") when he was sure he heard the little gate outside the Johnsons' front door make an *eeep* sound. Freddie paused in the center of the living room, as if he were playing musical chairs and someone had just stopped the track. His right foot was slightly off the ground, his left hand was by his side, and his right was hovering around his face about to scratch his nose.

Clunk.

The gate closed.

The mailman had already been by; it couldn't be him. Freddie stepped closer to the hallway. He could see people-shaped silhouettes through the semi-opaque window at the top of the front door. He whirled around in a panic and grabbed his backpack, then, just as a key was inserted into the lock, he darted into the bit of the hall that led to the bedrooms and shut the dividing door, buying himself a few extra moments.

Instinctively, Freddie dove into Violet's room and ran to the double doors that led to the courtyard. Neither would open. He looked around, his heart thudding faster and faster in his chest. Nothing. Nowhere to hide. Then, he noticed a hatch in the ceiling above Violet's bed. The attic? He didn't have time to look for the pole that would open it, so he clambered on top of the short, thick bookcase at the end of the bed.

His clumsy feet sent a perfume bottle flying with a soft thud onto the carpet. No time to pick it up. He stretched up and, with fingers that only just about reached, managed to undo the clasp so that the hatch dropped down into the room. Freddie threw his backpack up into the hole, then bent his knees and propelled himself upward. He managed to grab hold of the side of the opening and dangled there for a moment. Then, with every ounce of strength he could summon, he pulled himself up through the ceiling.

* * *

He was breathing so hard and his fingers were trembling so much that he thought he might pass out. He was crouched over the hatch, holding it in place because Violet had entered her room before he'd had chance to fumble with the clasp. Around him, the attic was pitch dark. But then, as his eyes adjusted, dotted around his enclosure he saw clustered pinpricks of light coming from air vents in the floor.

From a vent above Violet's room, he heard the tap of the perfume bottle as she replaced it on the bookcase. He held his breath, waiting for her to scream, "Mum! Someone's been in my room!" but she didn't. And then her door closed.

As the Johnsons settled back in, their presence filtered up through the ceiling. A bizarre concoction of sounds that made Freddie realize just how quiet it had been while he was there on his own. From the cluster of light above the kitchen, he heard Violet's mother say, "I can't believe you left this here for an entire three weeks." She'd noticed the buttery knife. Crap. His value-brand coffee was in the cupboard along with his long-life milk. He'd finished his cornflakes that morning too and put the box in the garbage. Crap, crap, crap.

"It wasn't three weeks, though, was it?" Violet snarked back.

"Yes, but you didn't know that, Violet. As far as you—"

Pete Johnson interrupted his wife and daughter. "Come on you two, it's been a long couple of days. Knock it off, yeah? And, Vi, be nice to your mother; she's had a hard time."

There was no response from Violet; perhaps she had rolled her eyes.

Freddie took the opportunity, knowing Violet was definitely in the kitchen, to twist the clasp back in place and release his grip on the hatch. The air smelled of dust and oldness. It made his skin prickle. He sat up, scooted backward, and bumped up against a pile of cardboard boxes. He would have to wait here until they went out. What day was it? Would there be work tomorrow? School? Damn, it was Friday. Freddie tried to ignore the twang of panic in his chest. Monday. He could be here until Monday. He mentally catalogued the contents of his backpack. There was probably a bottle of water lingering at the bottom but nothing edible.

"I'll call H," Ellie Johnson was saying. "I'm sure she'll give me and Jamie a lift until I can drive."

"It could be months," said Pete.

"She won't mind."

"You shouldn't have gone on that slope—Hugh said you weren't ready."

"Don't start, Pete."

Silence.

Then Ellie said, "You'll have to go shopping. I'll make you a list."

"Great."

Violet was back in her room. Freddie heard a couple of switches flick on and off as something was plugged into a socket. A phone charger? Laptop? The courtyard doors clunked open, and Freddie pictured Violet's ribbony curtains blowing in the breeze. Then, the soft beat of music he'd never heard before began to vibrate through the attic boards. Freddie pressed his palm to the hatch and smiled as she began to sing.

But his smile didn't last long; after a couple of hours tracing the Johnsons' movements from room to room, Freddie's bladder was aching. Violet was still listening to music, so he retrieved the bottle from his backpack, downed the remaining slurp of water, then peed into the empty plastic container as quietly as he could. If it hadn't been so desperately uncomfortable, it would have been funny.

It was too dark to move much farther away from the hatch; Freddie was too afraid of knocking something over and making a noise that would be heard down below. So, he slept. Occasionally, he woke, registered that the Johnsons were still moving about, then dozed off again.

It was late, because there was no longer any light at all and Violet's music had been turned off when he heard her crying. At first, he wasn't sure it was crying. So, he stomach-shuffled toward the vent above her room and strained his ears. What could she be crying about? Maybe there was a boyfriend? Maybe they had broken up?

Eventually, the crying stopped. But Freddie spent the rest of the night with his cheek to the floor, wishing he'd been able to say, "Don't worry—whatever it is, it'll be all right."

# 7
## FREDDIE

For twenty-four hours Freddie barely moved. Eventually, though, he felt brave enough to venture deeper into the attic. He moved, bit by bit, away from the hatch and managed to stretch out between what was either box-es or suitcases. He wriggled his shoulders against the plywood floor. He even cleared his throat once or twice because if he hadn't the itch would have ascended into a coughing fit.

For Freddie, each minuscule noise was amplified by the congealed darkness surrounding him and each one made his heart punch harder in his chest. But, slowly, he realized that no one could hear him. The daily hum of the kettle being boiled, cupboards opening, the TV, the radio, the doorbell, the next-door neighbor's dog... they drowned him out. Slowly, Freddie realized that Violet Johnson and her family had absolutely no idea there was a stranger living above them.

Despite this knowledge, he remained careful. He waited until Violet's music was particularly loud or until she ventured into the kitchen before he did noisier things like pee or sneeze. And each time she left, he listened for the front door or for an indication that the family were going out. But for the entire weekend, one or all of the Johnsons stayed at home. And Freddie was trapped.

* * *

By Saturday evening, he had to force himself to take long deep breaths and hum music in his head because the darkness was giving his thoughts too much room to run free. Memories were clambering at the sides of his skull, trying to get in. He tried to think of other things— of the money he'd saved and what he could do with it, even though things hadn't worked out as planned. But he couldn't. So, he focused on the Johnsons and the music in his head and, finally, on Sunday afternoon, he managed to locate the light switch.

He had been methodically snaking his fingers along the sloping wooden joists above his head and finally came across it on a section close to the hatch that he could have sworn he'd already examined.

When he flicked the switch, he was momentarily blinded by the harsh white light that flooded the space around him. After some furious blinking, the blindness subsided, and Freddie was able to assess his situation properly for the first time. The Johnsons' attic was huge. It mirrored the entire square-footage of the bungalow except maybe Ellie and Pete's room, which seemed like an extension. Box-less nooks were dotted all around him where things had been shifted this way and that or shoved on top of one another. And he could now see that the holes in the floor were part of an extinct ventilation system that had been disconnected, its tubes and pipes and wires piled in the far corner of the attic.

Freddie needed to do two things: he needed to conceal himself in case someone stuck their head through the hatch unexpectedly, and he needed to find something to occupy his mind so he wasn't left solely with his own thoughts. But perhaps because he liked her music or perhaps because he didn't want to feel too far away from his only escape route, he also wanted to remain close to Violet's room.

So, behind a cluster of boxes labelled *XMAS*, Freddie made himself a more comfortable place to hide. Inside a big, black suitcase with wonky wheels, he found a padded sleeping bag that he stretched out like a mattress. Then he emptied the contents of his backpack and lined up his things around him: another nearly empty bottle of water, a cereal bar he'd forgotten about, two pairs of unwashed pants, his now very crumpled suit, and his posh shoes.

These actions, which would have taken minutes under normal circumstances, took Freddie over an hour. It was as if he was moving in slow motion. Or playing that Operation game he'd had when he was younger — terrified that if he made a wrong move an alarm would start screeching.

Finally finished and having indulged in the light for

what he considered far too long, Freddie was about
to turn it off when he spotted a box labelled *MUM'S
BOOKS.* It was small and balanced on top of an empty
car-seat box. Carefully, he lifted it down to his makeshift
bed and opened it.

The books that were inside were what Freddie considered to be "old person" books. The kind he always
caught Madge reading when the shop was quiet. They
didn't look like the sort of books Ellie would read.
Perhaps they had belonged to someone else's mum.
Either way, he was thankful for something to look at
that wasn't just floor and boxes. So, he allowed himself a few more minutes with the light and opened the
least romantic looking of the books, one with a Navy
SEAL and a battleship on the front. Two short chapters
in, Freddie realized that it was nowhere even close to
a book about military history, but he kept reading anyway because it was distracting him from the grinding
hunger in the pit of his stomach.

He was midway through chapter three when a clatter-
ing noise from downstairs jolted him back to reality. He
thought it was the sound of Violet opening her courtyard
doors, but he hadn't been paying attention. It could have
been someone fetching a ladder, erecting it below the
hatch, getting ready to come and deposit their vacation
suitcases. As quietly and quickly as he could, he flicked
off the light and crouched on the corner of his sleeping
bag, head ducked behind the boxes.

It wasn't a ladder. It was Violet. Had she left through
her courtyard, or was she simply letting in some fresh
air? The doors clattered again. Closed this time.
Freddie waited for her music to start playing or for

the clunk of her phone charger being jammed into a socket. There was nothing. Then, Ellie's voice. "Pete! Violet's gone."

Pete's reply was muffled and came from somewhere else in the house.

"I don't know. Probably to see Aisla."

Pete was closer now but still unintelligible.

"My ankle, Pete. I can't drive."

"Fine. I'll go."

"Well, I'm coming with you."

"We don't both need to go, Ellie."

"I'm coming. I'll get Jamie."

And, just like that, the bungalow was empty.

Freddie's legs felt suddenly tingly, as if he'd been sitting with them crossed for too long. He couldn't make himself move. For a long moment, he just sat on his sleeping bag, chin on his chest, heart pulsating faster and faster and louder and louder by the second. Why had Violet snuck out? Was she grounded? He hadn't heard any arguments. Perhaps something had happened on vacation...

He shook his head and punched himself lightly on the thigh. This was his chance to get out, and he was wasting it. Quickly, he shoved his things back into his bag, unfastened the hatch, and allowed it to swing down into Violet's room. Then he lay flat on his stomach and peered over the edge. Her bedroom was empty.

Two swift but shaky movements and Freddie was on Violet's bookcase, then the floor beside her bed. Unlike when they were on vacation, her room now looked thoroughly inhabited. Clothes were strewn in piles around the room, emanating from a half-unpacked suitcase that sat mouth-open in front of the wardrobe. Freddie lingered in the middle of the room. To his right, the courtyard doors. The key was there, in the lock. He could easily slip out, climb over the wall, and be gone.

But he didn't.

Instead, he went to the kitchen and siphoned off some cookies, some tinned apricots, and half a loaf of bread that he'd remembered was in the back of the freezer. He threw away the nearly overflowing pee bottle he'd tucked in his back pocket, grabbed an empty Coke bottle from the recycling bin, and filled it with tap water.

Okay. He was ready. He had enough supplies to last a few days at least—to help him eke out the money he'd saved while the Johnsons had been away. Maybe he could buy a tent; he knew people who'd done that and found somewhere secluded to set it up, so at least they had somewhere to sleep and wash. Yes. A tent could work...

He couldn't leave through the back gate because he'd need the key for that and there'd be no way of returning it. So, taking one last look around the kitchen, and putting a couple more pounds in the rainy-day jar to ease his conscience, he went back through the lounge and the hall to Violet's bedroom.

He should have left. Any sensible person would have. But when he put his hand on the door handle and pulled it toward him, cold air bled through the gap and down his arm and he remembered what it was like before. All that time before. He thought of the list of rooms he'd seen on the Johnsons' TV because, realistically, how long would it be before he was asked to take his tent and move or before someone stole it or destroyed it?

Most of the rooms he saw had even been furnished. He'd have his own bed, his own wardrobe, his own address. And then he thought of Violet. He barely even knew what she looked like, but he knew that if he left, he would never be this close to her again.

So, for the second time, Freddie stayed.

# 8

## VIOLET

Sneaking out of the house had been stupid. It was something Old Violet would have done. New Violet was supposed to be more sensible, but her mum had asked
her to stay put and she'd been desperate to see Aisla.
After their messages on vacation, she could feel her life
bleeding away like a painting soaked in too much water.
And she was going to do all she could to keep it tangible.
Which meant, first, going to Aisla's and seeing her face to
face. If she couldn't persuade her to ditch the no-texting
rule, at least she'd be able to get her landline number.

When her mum and dad caught up with her halfway
there, however, they bundled her back into the car and
pointed out that all she'd needed to do was ask and
they'd have given her the number. But Violet hadn't
thought of that.

Her mum had tried to be sympathetic, especially when

Violet explained about her friends practically ghosting her. But they had still argued. Her mum reminded her that the reason they had moved her to Briar Ridge in the first place was to try and get rid of this kind of behavior. That they thought she'd changed. Her mum even threw in, "Are you trying to punish us, Vi? Is that what this is? You're mad because we can't afford to keep you there, and you're showing us what's going to happen when you go back to a normal school?"

That wasn't it. In all honesty, Violet hadn't thought it through as much as that. But she wasn't devastated that it had made them feel guilty. Despite knowing it wasn't her parents' fault, she would have liked a little acknowl-edgment from them that the process of moving schools wasn't going to be easy for her.

They didn't ground her. But they made it clear that if she did it again, they would, so she asked careful per-mission before catching the bus into town the next day.

"Why do you need to go into town?" her dad asked, bluntly.

"Arnhurst doesn't make older students wear uniforms. I need something to wear."

Her dad raised an eyebrow. "You've got a wardrobe— actually, a floor—full of clothes."

Violet didn't reply. She was trying to decide whether to respond or sulk back to her room when her mum intervened.

"All right, Vi. Take a twenty from my purse."

Her dad looked up from his laptop. "Seriously, Ellie? You're rewarding her for bad behavior. You know that?"

Her mum was trying to keep her voice calm and mea-sured, and Violet felt the heat rising in her cheeks for having caused another argument.

"Pete, it's different for girls than it is for boys. You can't just throw on a pair of jeans and a Tee-shirt. Violet wants to make a good impression." Her mum glanced over at Violet, clearly hoping that what she'd said had proved both her in-depth understanding of teenage girls and that she didn't bear a grudge for last night.

"You know what? Do what you want. You always do." Her dad slammed his laptop shut, tucked it under his arm, and stomped off.

Violet sighed. She was on the verge of tears and trying not to be. Somehow, she'd convinced herself that the vacation would fix them. But it hadn't.

Her mum squeezed her arm, still unnaturally cheerful. "Don't mind him, love, he's just—"

"Stressed. Yeah."

"Don't miss your bus." Her mum motioned to the door. Violet almost didn't want to go because she knew her parents would now spend most of the morning arguing; they tended to forget that although Jamie didn't speak, he could still hear perfectly well. She should probably have taken him with her. But she didn't. She just grabbed her bag and her sketchbook and left.

* * *

When Violet had first realized that her new school was non-uniform, she'd been delighted. Finally, no more navy tights or pleated skirts. But then it had dawned on her that the outfit she chose for her first day at Arnhurst would define her for the entirety of her time there. Her new classmates would form an instant opinion of her based almost solely upon what she wore.

She remembered a conversation she'd had with Aisla a couple of months ago. They'd been surfing the magazine rack in Waitrose, waiting for Aisla's au pair to finish the shopping, when Aisla had pointed to a picture of Kate Thingy from that reality show. Kate Thingy had dyed her hair a pale shade of purple. "That would look amazing on you, Vi," Aisla had said. Violet had asked her whether it wouldn't be a little bit silly to match her hair to her name, but Aisla had said, "Are you kidding? It would be totally meta."

Now, standing in the hair-dye aisle of Superdrug, Violet took out her phone and googled the definition of *meta*. Google told her it was "something referring to itself," which didn't really seem to relate to hair color, but she couldn't help thinking that purple hair could send out exactly the right message: cool, arty, on-trend but individual at the same time.

Violet grabbed the box of pastel dye and took it up to the counter. She threw in a new eyeliner and a plump-up-your-lashes mascara too. When she got home, she dove straight into the bathroom, where she studied the instructions on the box and followed them to the letter. She couldn't afford for her hair to go green, but at least if she colored it now, she'd have a fortnight to fix it if it all went horribly wrong.

The dying process took about twenty minutes, after which Violet returned to her room to dry her hair. Wet, it didn't look much different from normal. But as it dried it took on the appearance of one of those love-heart candies that Jamie always smiled at. Not quite as purple as the picture on the box but way more original than plain old blonde.

When her mum called her for dinner, Violet braced herself for the impeding argument. Her mum had given her money to go shopping and gotten into a fight with her dad on her behalf. Some time when Violet was out, her dad had left the house and still wasn't back. This would not go down well.

Hoping confidence would win their mum over, Violet entered the kitchen in a flourish and slid straight into a chair beside Jamie. He turned his face up at her and raised his podgy fingers to stroke a strand of her hair. Balancing on her crutches, their mum placed a bowl of salad in the center of the table, dished up three portions of lasagna, and took a seat opposite them. Then she noticed. Her jaw twitched. Violet looked down at her plate and prodded the lasagna with her fork. But then their mum cleared her throat and said, "I like it."

Violet raised her eyes to study her mother's face. "You do?"

"Mm, it's like that woman...what's her name? The one from TV?"

Violet was stunned.

"Is it permanent?" Their mum was trying to sound casual, as though she was merely curious rather than praying it would wash out.

"Semi."

Their mum smiled. Her shoulders relaxed, and she started to eat her lasagna, gesturing to Violet to do the same. Jamie waved his fork at the place where their dad usually sat.

"Daddy's working late, sweetheart. We'll save him some food though, don't worry."

For a moment, Violet didn't say anything. But then she couldn't help it. "If he works for himself now, how come he's always so late? It wasn't like this before."

Their mum didn't look up, didn't even blink. "We've been away, Vi; he's got lots to catch up on."

"But he—"

"Jamie, would you like a yogurt? Vi, be a love and get your brother a yogurt."

Violet crossed her knife and fork. "Sure."

# 9
## FREDDIE

After Violet had left for town, Ellie and Pete argued. Loudly. Freddie didn't need to strain his ears to hear them. In fact, he found himself trying *not* to hear them. It reminded him of the times his dad and Janet had argued. His father had always been drunk and Janet had always tried, in her thin willowy way, to calm him down. She'd rarely been successful.

Pete wasn't drunk. But the argument went the way all arguments do and suddenly it wasn't about Violet going into town; it was about Ellie not understanding the pressure he was under. And then it was about Pete not being sympathetic enough to the children—or to Ellie. About him hardly noticing that she'd broken her damn ankle.

"I'm starting to think there's someone else, Pete. That's what I'm thinking. Do you even care?"

Freddie jammed his fists over his ears and buried

his face into his sleeping bag. When his dad and Janet had argued like this, he'd always left the house. He hadn't stayed and held Amy's hand, made sure she was okay, played games with her so she didn't hear. No. Freddie had always left; walking for hours and dreaming of the day he would have a car and be able to drive away from them.

After he'd finally gotten his license, he'd actually felt excited when the first row started. He couldn't wait to grab his dad's car keys and wheel-spin out of the drive. He remembered Amy following him into the hall, her tiny voice. "Freddie?"

The memories were coming thick and fast, a tsunami of images he couldn't stop.

Getting in the car, keys in the ignition, music cranked up, no mirror checks, no need, only the driveway, feet on pedals.

*SLAM.*

Silence.

Pete had left, pulling the front door violently shut on his way out. Ellie was crying, Violet wasn't back yet, and Freddie felt that if he stayed in the attic a moment longer, he would suffocate under the weight of his own thoughts.

"Jamie, come on. We're going to Aunt Helen's." Ellie was trying to sound cheerful, probably mopping her cheeks and blotting her eyes as if Jamie hadn't heard everything she and Pete had been saying.

A few moments later, the front door clicked shut. Leaving his things where they were, Freddie jumped through the hatch and landed as softly as he could on Violet's bedroom floor. For a moment, he stood with his hands braced on his knees, taking deep conscious breaths and trying to slow his heartbeat. He needed to get out, needed air. But if he left and couldn't get back in, he would be saying goodbye to his one chance of changing things.

In the days before the family returned, he'd earned one hundred and forty pounds in his suit. It was in his pocket now. He could feel it. A mixture of notes and coins wedged beside his thigh.

A voice in his head was taunting him, and he needed to find a way to make it stop. *Don't you remember what you did?* Freddie grabbed hold of his hair and shook his head violently. He remembered, of course he did. But he needed to believe he could be something better.

He looked up, focusing on Violet's drawings. He homed in on the one of a mountain with a lake beneath it and stars in the sky. As he looked closer, he saw birds in the trees around the lake and a fish jumping out of the water. He kept looking until his breathing returned to something closer to normal, and then he sat down on the edge of Violet's bed. He needed to think clearly. With the family there, his plan became more difficult, of course it did, but it could still work. It had to work. He would just have to be organized, methodical, not take any chances, and not let himself become overwhelmed by his own thoughts.

Standing up, he borrowed a pen from Violet's desk and took a crumpled piece of paper from her trash, then went to the kitchen. Luckily, it seemed that Ellie was a stickler for updating the calendar. She had already amended it, writing in white-out on top of the days that were previously blacked out for their vacation.

Freddie unfolded his piece of paper, drew a grid on the empty side, and set about labeling the most important events. Ellie was back at work in two days' time, and Jamie was back at school then too. Violet, however, didn't start back until Monday the twenty-ninth— two weeks from now. The calendar said *Vi New School*, which probably went part way to explaining the crying and the sneaking out. The only regular event was *Jamie, ST* at 4:00 p.m. every Tuesday. What was *ST*?

Pete was the anomaly. The wild card. His actions and movements weren't listed on the calendar. Yesterday, despite the fact it was Sunday, and they should still have been on vacation, he had left home at 7:00 a.m. and returned at 7:00 p.m. Freddie had no idea where he went, and it seemed Ellie didn't either. She'd asked, "What's on the agenda today, then?" But she had been met with an evasive answer that revealed precisely nothing.

Freddie hovered by the kitchen table. He was desperate to just sit for a moment. Make himself a cup of tea. Look out of the kitchen window at the Johnsons' garden with its old-fashioned concrete birdbath and rusty swing seat. But it was risky. Too risky. So he returned to his boxes and his sleeping bag.

\* \* \*

Staring at his scribblings—his hurried, sketchy annotation of the Johnsons' movements—Freddie turned them over to see what was on the other side of the paper he'd borrowed. It was a poem, written in Violet's loopy round handwriting:

*Behind my eyes, you smell of lavender.*
*You are soft hands and yellow sweaters.*
*Behind my eyes, you wear red scarves.*
*You are wrinkles and smiles.*

*Behind my eyes, you're still here.*

Freddie shivered. Had Violet written this herself? He didn't recognize it, but the only poetry he'd ever read had been war poems at school. He pressed his fingertips to the page as if the words themselves might tell him who'd written them. And as he did, a deep, aching sense of "What the hell am I doing?" lodged itself in Freddie's gut.

Until now, the things he'd taken from the Johnsons had been utterly impersonal—food that was about to be thrown away and water from their taps. But this was a piece of Violet. This was something she hadn't meant anyone to see. And up in their ceiling, through the vents in the floor, he was hearing things the Johnsons' didn't intend for anyone to hear. He was living in their attic. Listening to their conversations. Sneaking in and out and around, totally unnoticed. It was the stuff of nightmares. If they knew. If they found out...

Freddie could feel himself sliding again. His black cloud was descending, and he felt utterly helpless. As it always did, the helplessness turned into panic. Air swelled uncomfortably in his chest, his skin fizzed, and his eyes watered. He had become a ghost, and the Johnsons' attic was his purgatory. He couldn't leave because he still desperately wanted to see his plan through—wear the suit, save the money, be someone, meet Violet (not part of his original plan but now rapidly becoming the most important part). But staying... Was staying really any better than sleeping on the street?

Just as he was beginning to think the answer was no, Violet's door banged shut and she turned on her music. It was a song he'd listened to before. He'd probably even danced to it once. A slow dance, with a girl whose name he couldn't remember, at a party full of people he hadn't spoken to since he left. But Violet's version of the song wasn't the one he knew. It was an ethereal, acoustic cover, sung by a man and a woman. Their voices seeped into his skin, trickled down his arms and legs, and he felt his body relaxing.

The music played on, and Freddie kept listening. Each day, Violet played something he hadn't heard before. And for over a fortnight, even though he barely made it out of the attic, he didn't mind because he felt as if he was getting to know her.

In the mornings, the songs she played were upbeat. Perhaps from the charts—he wouldn't know. His favorite was the one with the French rap in the middle of it. Every time, she sang along, clumsily but with gusto, often putting the song on repeat until Ellie shouted, "Change the record, Vi!"

In the afternoons, when he imagined she was sketching in her egg chair, she played songs without words. And in the evenings her playlists became melancholy. Until now, Freddie hadn't realized how much he missed having music in his life. For the first few weeks after his dad and Janet had left him, he'd kept his phone and charged it up in cafés, plugged his earbuds into his ears, and drowned out the world as he wandered aimlessly. But then he'd used the last of his data and

couldn't afford to top it up, so he'd taken it to the second-hand electronics shop at the sketchy end of town
and accepted twenty pounds for it. Since then, the only
music he'd heard was other peoples'—in shops, at the
shelter, snippets from car windows or pubs.

Occasionally, Gina from the Pay What You Can Kitch-
en had let him choose songs from her phone when he
helped her clean up after closing. But the choice had
always been limited to things with too much bass and
not enough voice.

Gina. He had almost forgotten her. She was his only
friend, although Freddie had always suspected she'd
like to be a little more than just friends. They had encountered each other sporadically during his first few
months on the street, and then one night they had both
ended up in the line at the youth shelter. There had only
been ten beds available, and Freddie had been ahead
of Gina in the line. Counting back, Freddie had realized
she was number eleven. So, he'd given her his spot and
opted to spend the night outside in a sleeping bag so
that she didn't have to.

After that, Gina had introduced him to the Kitchen,
where she volunteered, and made sure to give him ex-
tra-big portions, even when he couldn't pay as much
as ten pence toward his meal. He'd gone there every
Tuesday and Thursday without fail, and now he had
disappeared without saying a word. Gina knew he'd
been finding things hard since the shelter had closed.
She'd be worried.

Freddie contemplated sneaking out the next day and
going to see her. The Johnsons were going for lunch to
celebrate Violet's impending new school, so he'd have

time to sneak in and out. But how would he explain himself? Where would he say he'd been? If he told her the truth, Gina wouldn't understand. She'd rather sleep in a doorway than do what he was doing. She'd think it was creepy, weird, and dangerous. Even if he tried to explain, she'd tell him he'd lost his mind. She'd say there must be another way...

No, he would wait until later. When he could surprise her and tell her how well he was doing. Offer her a spot on his sofa for the night if she needed it.

Freddie fell asleep that night imagining Gina's face when he told her he'd gotten his own place, calculating how many days he would need once he was back in his suit in order to save two months' rent, and listening to a song with plonky guitars and an odd amount of whistling.

# 10

## VIOLET

The day had finally arrived. Day Zero. Violet's first day at Arnhurst. She'd set her alarm for six-thirty and tried on four different outfits before settling on skinny jeans, an oversized white shirt tied with a thin leather belt, her tan boots, a chunky cardigan, and her new eyeliner. Her mascara was purple to match her hair.

Her mum greeted her with coffee and a cold omelet. "You'll be all right getting the bus?"

"It's the same one that goes into town. I'll be fine."

"All right, well, if you need anything just call me."

Violet nodded. "Is Helen picking you up?"

Her mum glanced at her watch. "Yes, in ten minutes. We're dropping Jamie at school on the way. You know which bus you need to catch?"

"The eight-ten. Mum, seriously, stop worrying."

Eventually, her mum and Jamie left the house, and

Violet was alone. More than anything in the world, she wished that she could stay here, cocooned, pretending nothing else existed. She longed for her dad's company car and Aisla's excited trill as they met at the school gates. She even missed her blazer.

Backpack on her shoulder, she braced herself as she opened the door, then took a deep breath and marched through. Confident, purple-haired Violet, who would make lots of friends and be insanely popular within minutes.

\* \* \*

She was not insanely popular within minutes. In fact, the instant she set foot on the bus, she regretted her hair. A gaggle of girls at the back narrowed their eyes at her as she moved down the aisle. Should she avoid them, or would they warm to her if she had the guts to approach? She had no idea about bus politics, and the pressure of deciding which seat to take meant she was still lingering when it started moving. She lurched forward, tripping over a nearby foot, and fell straight into the lap of a stranger.

Looking up, the stranger smiled. A boy. Perfect. He was insanely good looking, and Violet couldn't tell if he was smiling ironically or sincerely. The girls at the back were sniggering.

The boy glanced over his shoulder. "Don't mind them. Sit here if you like." He slid toward the window, making room. "I'm Chris."

"Thank you." Relief hummed on the surface of her skin. "Really. Thank you."

Chris laughed. "You're new?"

"Yes," she corrected her tone, diluted the poshness. "Yeah. Just starting. Today. I'm Violet."

"Well, don't worry, Violet," he winked. "I'll look after you."

Chris and Violet talked for the remainder of the bus ride. He was vacuous and probably only being nice to her because she was fresh meat but, all the same, she was grateful. As they disembarked, though, he merged with the gaggle from the back, and she wondered whether, the whole time, she'd been the butt of an inside joke.

Violet wasn't used to feeling this way. She was used to being one of the cool kids. She had shimmied around Briar Ridge with Aisla and the others as if no one could touch her. If they hadn't given up their phones, she could have texted and received words of wisdom. Support. Her own little cheerleaders in her pocket, that's what they'd said when she told them she had to go to Arnhurst. "Don't worry, Vi. We'll text you all the time. Like all day. Your own little cheerleaders in your pocket."

Yeah, right.

Violet was alone. And talking to Chris might have softened her embarrassment on the bus, but she had the feeling it had set her up as someone the back-seat girls would now deliberately dislike.

She knew she should have walked.

# NOVEMBER

# 11
## FREDDIE

Violet had been back at school exactly four days, and Freddie had missed her terribly. He had become so used to her presence in the room below him that now that she was gone, the quiet was deafening.

In the time between the Johnsons arriving home and Violet starting her new school, he had spent his days following her movements, listening to the family's conversations, and getting to know them. He had absorbed himself in their daily routines, as if he were reading a book he couldn't put down or binge-watching a TV series. He hadn't allowed himself to notice the darkness around him or the ache in his empty belly. He hadn't allowed his thoughts to take over or the flutter beneath his ribs to become panic.

Every now and then, he'd managed to sneak out and grab some food, stand by the window and drink up the daylight, wash himself at the bathroom sink because the shower would be too noisy and he might not hear them come home. But then he'd returned to the attic to wait.

Now, though, it was becoming harder and harder to stay in control; if he let himself think about what he was doing, his skin would begin to itch as if mites were burrowing at him from under the surface, his face would feel hot and clammy, and his breath would start to get quicker... But he needed to focus. He needed to remember *why* he was doing this. He needed to remember the plan, the room, the job.

But before he could venture away from the safety of the bungalow and start collecting money again, he also needed to be certain of the Johnsons' schedules. If he left and was unable to return, he'd lose everything: his money, his backpack...everything.

When the Johnsons had been on vacation, he'd caught the bus at nine and returned whenever he liked. But that wasn't going to work now that they were home. Now, he'd need to be back before they started to file in from work and school. Ellie and Jamie's movements weren't a problem; they conformed to the pattern etched on the calendar. And Pete was never home before seven. But Violet wasn't as easy to pin down. In theory, she should be home not long after Jamie and Ellie, but being in year twelve, her comings and goings could be infinitely more flexible than her parents' and her brother's. How many times had Freddie skipped school back when he saw it as an inconvenience rather than a luxury? Left early instead of staying for a study period? Faked a reading day?

The uncertainty of it all was almost enough to convince him that his plan was utter madness. But ever since he had scrolled through that list of rooms on the Johnsons' TV, he had been imagining his new life. And the more he'd imagined it, the more he'd *known*, deep down in the basement of his guts, that if he had his own place to live everything would change.

If he had his own space, he'd be able to distract himself from remembering. He'd be able to watch TV or read or listen to music, and his thoughts wouldn't get the better of him. He'd have somewhere to keep his clothes, so they'd stay clean and uncrumpled. He'd be able to sleep. Proper, deep sleep because he wouldn't be worried that someone was going to steal his things or tell him to move on. He'd be a person again, and he'd be able to find a job. It didn't matter what it was. He'd do anything. He had good grades and he was polite. Someone would hire him. And then maybe he'd bump into Violet somewhere and he'd have the courage to speak to her.

He just needed this one thing—the money to rent a room—and his life would start to go up instead of down.

He couldn't let the dream go, not yet. So, he told himself he would wait at least a week, until he was sure of Violet's movements, before stepping back into the suit. But then, on the Thursday of Violet's first week, he descended from the attic to gather supplies and found her planner sitting on her bed.

It was yellow and covered in clear plastic. It still looked new. Barely used. And when he opened it, there was none of the usual graffiti. No love hearts or scribbles or silly doodles. Just Violet's name and her timetable. She was taking art, of course, English, and math. That was a surprise; he hadn't imagined her as the mathematical type. Was she good at everything? Again, he sighed, feeling her slipping further and further out of his reach.

He was tempted to make a copy of her timetable, but he felt that might be a step too far, so he memorized it instead. She had several blocks of blank space between lessons but no free periods at the end of the day, which was good; she was less likely to come home early. And, since their argument about her sneaking out, she seemed to be trying to keep her parents happy, so he hoped this was enough to stop her from skipping an entire day.

He decided it was time. No more hanging around.

\* \* \*

The next morning, Freddie heard Pete leave the house, as usual, at seven, closely followed by Ellie and Jamie at seven-thirty, and Violet at eight-fifteen.

He waited until eight-thirty, to be sure she was one hundred percent gone, before he climbed down, tidied himself in the bathroom, and exited through the Johnsons' back door. He would be in time to catch the tail end of the morning rush, but he would need to be back before Violet, Jamie, and Ellie started to trickle home, which meant only five hours of... What was he even doing? Begging? Hustling? That sounded better: hustling.

Five hours. Not as many as before and the plan would take longer to work, but it would still work. He was sure of it, and he felt the same sense of anticipation that he had when the idea had first come to him. Was he proud of what he was doing? No. But he had a purpose and a goal, and that was a lot more than he'd had a few weeks ago.

Riding the bus into town, he caught a glimpse of himself reflected in the window, and he almost believed that he was just a regular person on the way to a regular job. Before long, he was in position outside Costa Coffee. It was a gray morning. Drizzle clung to his jacket but, if anything, it added to his act—the sense of urgency when he patted at his pockets and said his first, "I'm so sorry; I've forgotten my wallet..." And as the day wore on and the weather worsened, and Freddie grew increasingly dejected in his appearance, the offers of help from well-meaning strangers became more and more generous.

Freddie was accepting a five-pound note and a pat on the arm from a man in a dark brown raincoat when he became very suddenly aware of someone watching him. The hairs on his neck tingled. His cheeks flushed. Out of the corner of his eye, he registered a woman-shaped silhouette pointed in his direction.

Thanking the man and turning toward the silhouette, Freddie knew instantly who the woman was. Her sharp edges and tightly crossed arms. Skin so white it looked as if it had been painted on. Pursed lips.

"Janet?"

Janet stepped back, raising her hands as she was being cornered in a darkened alley.

Freddie skirted around the people walking between them and found himself raising his own hands too, trying not to frighten her away.

For a moment, relief washed over him. The Freddie he was before his mum had died and his dad had started drinking, and before Janet and Amy and the street, came bursting back to life and a voice inside his head shouted, "You've found them! Everything will be okay. They never meant to leave you. They've tried hundreds of times to find you. You'll see. Just wait. She'll ask you to come home."

Freddie inhaled deeply, sucking air past his front teeth and down into his lungs. "You're still here. I thought you'd moved? It's...I'm really glad to see you." He was trying so hard to say the right thing, to not make her turn and walk away, that he couldn't seem to line his words up. "Is Dad here too?"

Janet's eyes narrowed. She bit her lip, then leaned forward. "Stay. Away."

And before Freddie could answer, she was gone. Once again, he was abandoned, stranded on the pavement, unable to move. His eyes began to sting. He blinked back the moisture that was biting at his eyelids and glanced up and down the main street. There were too many people. Too many bodies close to his. His throat tightened, his arms felt hot, and the heat quickly spread to his chest. He pulled at the top button of his shirt, trying to loosen it, but his fingers were too clunky. Feeling almost drunk, Freddie stumbled away from the crowds and found himself outside Madge's charity shop.

When he crossed the threshold, a bell jingled, and Madge looked up from behind the counter. She smiled, pleased to see him, but her smile quickly gave way to a concerned frown. "Freddie. You're as white as a ghost."

Freddie couldn't speak. His breath was coming too fast and the shop was spinning in and out of focus.

Madge started to walk toward him, and he tried to step forward, but his legs gave way. And then so did his consciousness.

* * *

When he came around, Madge was kneeling beside him. She helped him sit up and offered him a glass of water. His voice came out croakier than normal. "What happened?"

"Well, my love, seems you fainted. Don't you remember?"

Now he did. He remembered Janet, and he remembered the way she'd looked at him, and then he remembered why she'd looked at him that way, how it all began...

Madge lightly squeezed his shoulder. "Take it easy. Nice and slow." She bent to meet his eyes. "Concentrate on me, that's it...one...two...three..." She was breathing with him, in through her nose and out through her mouth.

A few minutes passed like that. Madge turned the sign on the shop door to Closed and sat beside him on the floor, not attempting to make him move until he finally looked up at her and said, "Thank you."

"Think you can stand up?"

Freddie nodded.

She guided him over to the chair behind the counter and made him sit. "Tea with sugar. That's what we need."

As he watched Madge make the tea, he wondered what she would say if he told her everything. Maybe she would she hug him and tell him it was okay, offer him a bed in her spare room, talk to her husband, explain they'd be taking Freddie under their wing for a while, help him back on his feet. Was this another way? A way that didn't involve lying and sneaking about and breaking into peoples' houses?

Madge pressed the warm mug into his hands and offered him a custard cream.

"Thank you," he said again.

She leaned on the counter opposite him. "Have you had panic attacks before?"

Freddie frowned. "Panic attacks?" So that's what it was. "Maybe..."

"My daughter used to get them when she was at school. The pressure."

"You have a daughter?"

"Three, actually, but Kat's the youngest. Twenty-seven. Still living at home though. She tells us she's forging a career as an 'influencer'? Whatever that means. She has ten thousand followers? I think that's good?" Madge laughed and pride twinkled in her eyes.

Freddie told her that ten thousand was very good, yes.

"Right, well, so far she's been given plenty of free clothes but doesn't seem to be making any money out of it. Apparently, that happens later." Madge shrugged. "What would I know? She's happy, that's the main thing. And we like having her with us, even if we are a bit cramped."

Freddie smiled and watched the daydream in which Madge became his surrogate mum float away in the wisps of steam from his tea.

"Now, Freddie. I'm far from an expert, but in my experience these things happen when you bottle your feelings up. It's your body's way of making you take notice of them. So, make sure you talk to someone, yes? About whatever's going on..."

He gave a half nod.

"Is there someone? Someone you can talk to?"

"Oh, yes. My girlfriend, Violet. She..." Lies. Again.

"Good. That's good." Madge glanced toward the door. She needed to re-open.

Freddie saved her from having to ask him to leave and stood up, quickly drinking the remainder of his too-sweet tea. "Madge, thank you, so much. But I've got to go."

"Of course," she looked at his suit. "Is the job going well?"

"It's great," he said, not quite looking her in the eye. "Really good. Thanks again."

"You're welcome. And if you do ever need someone to talk to, you know my door's always open." She turned the sign back and gave him a peck on the cheek. "And I always have custard creams."

Freddie was halfway through the door when Madge's voice called, "Oh, Freddie...wait. Just a second..."

He turned back. Was she going to say it? Was she going to tell him to come stay with her? Tell him they could make room. Tell him—

"I'm not sure if you'd be interested. Now that you've sorted yourself out, I mean. But my son-in-law, Grahaeme, he's a filmmaker..."

Madge was handing Freddie a thick, black business card. There was no phone number, just an email: *Grahaeme@GallowsFilms.com*.

"He's making a documentary, and he's looking for young people to talk to—" Madge cleared her throat as if what she was about to say was a swear word. "It's about homelessness in the community, particularly among teenagers like yourself."

"Oh, I see."

"I'm sure he'd be very interested to hear about your experiences, especially now you've turned things around, found a job..."

Freddie pocketed the business card and tried to look as if he meant it when he said, "I'll think about it. Thank you."

\* \* \*

By the time Freddie made it back to the main street, it was starting to get dark, the way it did on days like this. It was nearly three. He was cutting it close. So close, in fact, that he had barely shut himself back up in the attic and flopped down onto his sleeping bag when he heard Violet return.

All he'd been given before Janet had arrived was cash—seven pounds—and he hadn't had time to stop and buy anything or pilfer leftovers from the Johnsons. He had a cereal bar and an almost empty—and very flat—bottle of Coke in his bag. But that was it until morning and, as always, he had the nagging fear of being stuck for longer than expected.

He allowed himself half the cereal bar and a mouthful of Coke, then, hearing movement below, shuffled closer to the vent above Violet's room.

"Violet, guess who's here to see you?" Ellie's cheerful voice from the doorway.

Freddie pictured Violet looking up from her floating chair, the place he always pictured her, and beaming.

"Aisla!"

A girly squeal traveled from one side of the room to the other, followed by a string of gabbled questions and answers that flowed so quickly Freddie could barely keep up with them. Finally, they slowed down, and the voice he guessed was Aisla's said, "So, you're Queen Bee already, right?"

Violet paused. "Not exactly. I think the hair was a mistake."

"Shut up. Your hair is perfection."

"No. I mean. It's okay. Arnhurst, I mean. It's not as bad as I thought it'd be. But it's not like being with you guys."

Freddie wondered whether Aisla noticed that Violet wasn't really answering her question. She didn't seem to. "God, Vi. I know. Daisy and Patts are great, but it's not the same. Three just isn't as good as four."

"I'm sorry." Violet sounded truly apologetic.

"Not your fault, is it? Anyway, maybe your dad's consulting thing will work out and you'll come back. Like, next year or something?"

"Yeah. Maybe."

"So. Listen. I was thinking. Tomorrow night?"

Violet's tone brightened. "Fireworks? I can't tell you how good it'll be to see everyone. Where are we doing it? I tried calling you for details the other night, but you weren't in. This no-text thing is super annoying by the way—"

"Yeah. Thing is, Vi. We thought probably it's better if it's just us Briar Ridge crew. Everyone will be talking about school stuff, and you're just going to feel super awkward since you don't really know what's going on anymore and—"

"Aisla, it's only been a few weeks. I think I'll be able to keep up."

Freddie wasn't sure if Violet sounded annoyed or hurt, but he felt pretty sure he wanted to kick Aisla in the shins and tell Violet not to waste her time with someone so vapid.

"'Course you would, but, you know, Dais and Patts agree and, yeah..." Aisla trailed off. She wasn't asking Violet. She was telling her: you are not one of us anymore, and you're not welcome.

"Right."

"We'll do something soon though, yeah?"

"Uh-huh."

Aisla's voice headed for the door. "Okay. Loveyou-byeee."

# 12
## VIOLET

Violet was tempted to show up at the clandestine Briar Ridge fireworks just to spite Aisla. To show off her new hair, and laugh, and be the life and soul of the party. But then her mum told her that her dad, for once, wasn't working and asked if the four of them could go to the local display together. The way she asked, and the way Jamie grinned and made firework puffs with his fingers, tugged at Violet's conscience. And so, maybe to make amends for sneaking out, she decided to go with them.

The town display had historically been at the football stadium. But when the council had banned the bonfire a few years ago it had moved to the park. Without the bonfire, it was a shrunken, muted version of what Violet remembered from when she was younger. But Jamie liked the lights and the cotton candy stalls, and her dad waited for half an hour for hot dogs that cost five pounds each without moaning about it, so that was nice.

Violet was shuffling her feet in her boots and biting down on her hot dog when someone tapped her shoulder. She turned, hot dog and bun wedged between her front teeth, and found Chris from the bus towering over her. She hadn't spoken to him since because he had turned up the very next day in a black VW with orange stripes down the side. She'd heard some girls whispering that he was the first in their year to pass his test. So, no more bus for him.

Violet thanked God that it was dark because hopefully he couldn't see her cheeks turning to molten lava and the ketchup that she was pretty sure had oozed onto her chin.

"Hi, new girl." His voice dripped with confidence.

Violet swallowed a too-big chunk of hot dog. "Hi."

"Haven't seen you around much."

She was regaining her composure now and caught herself flicking her hair and widening her eyes as she said, "I heard you passed your driving test?"

Chris broadened his shoulders and nodded. Violet hadn't realized it was possible to nod with a swagger, but he did.

"Maybe you could take me for a ride sometime?" What was she saying? The words were just falling out of her mouth, and she couldn't seem to stop them.

"Give me your number. I'll text you." A demand. Not a question.

Violet quickly tugged off the fingerless glove her grandmother had knitted her and shoved it into her pocket. Chris handed her his phone, and she tapped in her number. Then, just like that, he was gone, melding with a cluster of girls and boys she thought she recognized as being in her year.

"Who was that?" Her mum was at her shoulder.

"Just a guy from school."

"He seemed nice?"

"I guess. I don't really know him."

\* \* \*

Later that night, Violet was closing her laptop and finally giving in to sleep when her phone lit up. *Let me know when you're free, new girl. Can't wait to take you for a ride.*

# 13

## VIOLET

The Wednesday after fireworks night, her dad surprised her mum with a very unexpected date night. So unexpected that although her mum seemed initially thrilled, her smile soon changed into something more suspicious.

"It was one of those last-minute things," he said. "You don't want to go?"

"Of course, Pete, it's wonderful. It's just...why?"

Violet looked down at her phone as her dad wrapped his arms around her mum's waist and kissed her neck. She couldn't remember the last time she saw her parents being affectionate with each other.

"Because you deserve it. Because I've been horrible to live with and the vacation was ruined, and I just thought..." He sighed. "I'm trying to be better at this, El."

Violet didn't know what he meant by "this", but her mum smiled properly after he said it. "What about...?"

She turned to look at Violet and Jamie.

"All sorted. Jamie's going to sleep over at Aunt Helen's and, Vi, we're trusting you not to have a rave and wreck the place—okay?"

Her parents had never left her alone overnight. *Never.* Violet looked up from her phone and nodded, trying not to seem too enthusiastic. An hour later, her mum, dad, and Jamie set off, and Violet was left alone. Totally alone. It was only six. Her dad had bought her a frozen deep-crust pizza and had even put it in the oven for her before they left.

Violet turned on the TV, scrolled through Netflix, couldn't find anything she was in the mood for, and was just about to resort to her parents' ancient DVD collection when her phone pinged. *What you up to, New Girl?*

**Violet's thumbs hovered over the keyboard. She took** off her glasses. A knot had formed in her stomach, but she couldn't work out if it was excitement or nerves. Do it, she thought. *Home alone. Wanna come over?*

He replied almost instantly. *For sure. When?*

Violet glanced at the clock. *Seven? I have pizza and Netflix.* Wait. Did that sound like code for something? Had she just invited him over for sex? She felt a bit sick. *I love pizza. Send address. See you soon.*

* * *

He arrived at seven-thirty. Was he playing games or just genuinely tardy? Violet couldn't stand late people. But still, she gave him her best smile and ushered him inside, momentarily hoping her dad hadn't gotten around to installing those hidden cameras he'd threatened after they had been robbed last year.

He leaned against the door frame for a second before accepting her invitation, flexing his arm muscles and smoldering. He was so conventionally good looking that it had almost started to work in reverse, and Violet instantly started wondering what excuse she could make to get rid of him. He definitely wasn't there for pizza.

"Home alone, huh?"

Violet took a very deliberate glance at the clock on the wall in the hallway. "For a couple of hours, yeah."

Chris frowned. "Oh, right. I thought you meant, like, alone *all* night..."

Violet shrugged in what she hoped was a casual *Oh, sorry, I didn't mean to give you that impression* kind of way and walked through to the kitchen.

Chris followed her and, as she took the pizza out of the oven, he leaned on the counter behind her. "Got anything to drink?" He really did like to lean.

"Sure. Um. Coke?"

He made a sound that was almost a scoff. "A *real* drink?"

"Oh." She tried to stop her eyebrows arching. "Sure. Beer?"

* * *

Half an hour later, they were sitting side by side on the sofa. Chris hadn't eaten any pizza, which meant Violet hadn't either. He had, however, consumed three of her dad's 1664s. Violet was halfway through her first bottle and feeling a bit dizzy. As Chris droned on about having headshots taken for a potential modeling gig, she found herself nodding and trying not to keep looking sideways at the pizza. Her stomach was threatening to growl with hunger. Why on earth had she got herself into this situation? What had she expected? Sparkling conversation?

Chris put his beer bottle down on the coffee table—without using a coaster. Violet almost had to sit on her hands to stop herself from correcting it. Then he turned to her and snaked his arm around her shoulders. It was mostly resting on the back of the sofa, but then he started to inch toward her, and it dropped onto her neck. His arm was heavy, and a horrible second hand beer smell was snaking out from between his half-open lips.

Violet shuffled toward the armrest and patted his thigh in a manner she hoped implied "be seeing you, then".

He didn't move.

"Well, my parents will be back soon, so I guess..."

His face was so close to hers that she felt almost cross-eyed trying to look at him properly. "You said a couple of hours... We have time."

The arm that wasn't around her shoulders was now slung across her lap, his hand on her forearm.

He kissed her. It was not a good kiss. It was teeth and tongue and saliva, and his weight on her chest was stifling. She tried to push him up, laughing nervously. "Maybe next time, I really..."

His lips were on her neck now, but it was more biting than kissing. He tugged her ponytail, and suddenly she was totally underneath him and his hands were roaming everywhere. She started to shout. "Chris, I said no. Seriously..."

He wasn't stopping. Was he undoing her jeans? Panic rose in her chest, and all she could think was that he was so strong, so heavy. Then, all of a sudden, the weight was gone and a voice she'd never heard before was saying, "I'm pretty sure she said no."

She pushed herself up, tucking her knees under her chin and wrapping her arms around them. Her breath was quick; she felt dizzy. Chris was on the floor, and towering above him was a tall, ginger-haired boy with a face like thunder.

Chris was staggering to his feet and squaring up to the boy. "What the hell?!"

The boy stepped closer, mimicking Chris's body language and forming a barrier between him and Violet. "It's time for you to go." His voice was gruff, but something in it wavered. He was scrawny—Chris would definitely have won if it came to a fight between them, and Violet felt as if the ginger-haired boy was having to try very hard to come across as intimidating.

Chris stood stock still. Looking from Violet to the boy. Clearly trying to work out whether he should leave or throw a punch. After what felt like an almost comically long time, he pushed his chest into the boy's shoulder, shoving past him into the hall.

Just before he slammed the front door, he shouted back, "You're welcome to her—frigid bitch!"

The ginger-haired boy held up his palm, gesturing for Violet to stay still. "I'll check he's gone." She heard him lock the door, and then there was silence. Had he left too? Or had he just locked himself into the house with her, alone? Maybe she knew him? Was she having some kind of epic memory meltdown? She must have known him. He was in her house...

When he returned, he lingered in the doorway.

"I don't know you, do I?" she asked, standing up and trying to straighten her clothes.

"Um. No," replied the boy.

"Are you a burglar?" A chivalrous, almost good-looking, burglar.

"No. At least, I don't think so."

Violet swallowed hard; clearly, she'd swapped a horny, teenage rapist for a drug addict–burglar. Out of the frying pan and into the...

"I'm Freddie," he said, as if this was the answer to her question. "Are you...are you okay?"

Violet realized her cheeks were damp and swiped at the moisture with the back of her hand. "Yes."

He was studying her, looking at her straight on but in a soft, unintimidating kind of way. His eyes were a grayish shade of green.

"I'm Violet. Thanks for your help."

The boy named Freddie nodded. His hands were in his pockets, and his sleeves were rolled up. He didn't look like a criminal, and she couldn't see any marks in the crooks of his arms. But what did that mean? Simply that he didn't inject the drugs he used... Her thoughts were tripping over one another. Maybe he had just been walking past outside and had heard her shouting?

Suddenly, while she was still trying to decide whether she should be calling the police or not, she looked down at the untouched pizza and couldn't hold herself back any longer. "Sorry, I need to eat something." She sat back down on the sofa and grabbed the slice nearest to her. "Help yourself..."

The boy looked at her as if she was trying to lure him into a trap, glancing furtively at the doorway. She heard his stomach growl, loudly, and watched as he subconsciously licked his lower lip. She nudged the pizza box with her toe. "It's the least I can do."

Finally, he seemed to give in. He bobbed down in front of the coffee table and reached for the pizza. His fingers hovered above it for a moment, unable to decide which piece to take. When he settled on one, he ate it in three large bites and then returned for another. Mouth half full, he looked up and said, "Sorry, it's been ages... Thank you."

Ages since he ate? Or ages since he ate pizza?

Violet ate one more slice, then told him he could have the rest.

"Oh, no—thanks, but no. No, it's yours." He was standing again now, moving his weight almost imperceptibly from one foot to the other.

Violet leaned back on the sofa. She was ninety-nine percent sure she was losing her mind. There was a stranger in her house. She had no idea what he was doing there and, instead of asking him, or calling her parents or 9-9-9, she was sharing food with him. But the thing was, no matter how hard she tried to find it, there wasn't even a flicker of fear in her gut when she looked at him.

Even as she'd typed her invite to Chris, she'd known it was a bad idea. She had rationalized it, convinced herself that he was nice and had been kind to her and that if she made a good impression, he might tell the others she was *okay,* and she'd suddenly find herself with a friendship group. But she'd known it wouldn't go down that way. Her stomach, her skin, the dryness of her mouth, and the thickness of her tongue as she had welcomed him inside—they had all told her that he was *not* a nice boy.

But as she looked at her hungry, red-headed rescuer, she felt...curious, intrigued, safe.

She tucked a stray piece of hair back into her ponytail and closed the lid of the pizza box. Then she tilted her head to one side and said, "So, it's not that I'm ungrateful or anything, but—what are you doing in my house?"

# 14
## FREDDIE

His heart was going to burst right out of his chest. It was possible he was on the verge of a heart attack. The pizza that, a moment ago, had tasted so good now threatened a retaste on its way back up.

Violet was waiting for his answer. Her big cartoon eyes were staring at him. She didn't look scared, but her phone was on the armrest next to her and she was tapping the nail of her index finger on its screen. Probably getting ready to hit 9-9-9.

She looked at the window, gesturing to the street outside. "I thought maybe you'd heard something, but I'm pretty sure we have double glazing. So..."

Freddie scraped his fingers through his hair. He had three choices:

*Option 1.* Run away, and never come back—there was no way he'd be able to risk sneaking back in; they'd be on high alert after Violet revealed what happened.

*Option 2.* Make something up—but what? What could he possibly make up to explain this?

*Option 3.* Tell Violet the truth, and hope she was grateful enough for his help that she didn't call the police.

It had to be one or three. "It's, ah, a long story."

"Well," she quipped, "my plans for the evening were cut unexpectedly short, so I have time." She tucked her feet up underneath her and gestured for him to sit down.

Freddie took a deep breath and perched as far away from her as he could get. He couldn't look at her. "I've..." The words were stuck. Every muscle in his body tensed, bracing itself for impact. "I've been here a while."

"Here?" Violet looked around. "Like, in the house?"

He nodded. She thought he meant hours, not weeks.

"Did you think we were all out? Were you robbing us?"

"No. No, I wasn't. I'd never...I wouldn't."

Violet's forehead creased into a confused frown.

"I just needed somewhere to sleep."

The creases softened. But he hadn't told her all of it...

"The night you went skiing, I saw you leave. I was walking past. I didn't mean to—your notebook, it must have fallen out of your bag and got caught in the door, and I only meant to push it inside and shut it for you, but..." He was speaking quickly, trying to get it all out, trying to make her see that it had been an accident and it wasn't as horrendous as it sounded.

Violet's mouth had dropped slightly open, revealing a larger than normal gap between her front teeth, and she had folded her arms across her chest. She looked around as though she might spot where he'd been hiding, then she rolled her eyes and laughed. "Okay, very funny. Seriously though, if you're a burglar or something, I'm not going to call the police, not after you helped me. I just want to know..." She stopped. Then her eyes widened. "Ohmygod, you're serious."

Freddie nodded, and when she didn't scream or throw things or tell him to get out, he continued. He told her he didn't know what had made him come inside. He explained his plan to stay while her family was away and work to save money. He didn't say what work he had been doing. He told her about the money he had left in the rainy-day jar and how he hadn't watched television or slept in their beds. And he told her that when they'd returned home early, he'd panicked and hidden in the attic. And then he'd stayed. And now, four weeks had passed, and it was tonight.

By the time he finished his story, his mouth was dry, and his hands were clammy. He couldn't read the expression on Violet's face. She stood up and paced over to the window, clasping her phone, then back to the sofa. She didn't sit down. "You've been up there"—her eyes motioned to the ceiling—"this whole time?"

Freddie nodded.

She visibly shuddered. Obviously, she thought he was a creep. A psychopath. The whole idea of it was like something from a horror movie. Freddie tried to think of something to make it sound less awful. But what could he possibly say?

Violet was chewing her lower lip. "And where were you living before the attic?"

"Nowhere, I, um...nowhere."

She tilted her head to one side. He expected her to ask why, but she didn't.

Freddie picked the skin around his thumb. "I was supposed to be gone by now..." The sentence faded, and he wasn't sure how to finish it.

"But you stayed?"

"Yeah."

Violet nodded.

Freddie stood up and took a step toward the door, trying to look as unthreatening as possible. "I'll go," he said, the words stinging his throat.

"Go?"

"I'll get my things. You won't see me again, I promise."

"Just give me a minute to think," she said.

They were facing each other, and she was looking at him carefully. For the second or third time, Freddie saw her eyes dart down toward his arms.

"Do you take drugs?"

"No."

"Do you drink?"

"No. My dad's an alcoholic, so..." Why had he said that? She didn't need to know about his dad.

"What work are you doing?"

There was no point in lying, not now, so Freddie told her. He told her about the suit and the people who gave him coffees, sandwiches, muffins, ten-pound notes.

"Unbelievable," she said, almost a whisper.

"Honestly, I—"

"No. I believe you. I just mean it's unbelievable that people give more money to someone in a suit than to a...to a..."

"Than to someone who actually looks homeless?"

She nodded.

Freddie shrugged. "That's people, I guess."

"People are shit."

Not all people, he thought.

\* \* \*

Violet was pacing again, between the sofa and the window. "How long do you need? For your plan?" she asked, finally.

"If I save fifteen pounds a day, three weeks. Maybe a little longer now, um, now that you're all home. It's harder to get in and out—"

"All right."

He scanned her face, searching for a sign that it was a joke or a trap. "Why? I mean..."

"One good turn deserves another," she said, saving him from his stutter. "If you hadn't been here, who knows. And I believe that things happen for a reason. So, maybe you were meant to be here, and you were meant to help me, and now I'm meant to help you." She stopped and tucked a loose strand of hair behind her ear. It wasn't the blonde he'd seen when she left for vacation but a pale shade of purple.

"Thank you," he whispered.

# 15

## VIOLET

When she told him he could stay, she waited for the sensations of dread or fear or what-the-hell-are-you-doing-Violet to sink in. But they didn't.

The way he said thank you, it was as if his entire life depended on her. Probably, it did. She didn't have even the tiniest idea of what it was like to be homeless. To be alone. But whatever it was like, this boy would rather sleep locked in her family's attic than go back. And that, for now, told her all she needed to know.

Obviously, she should've called the police; it was what any normal, sensible person would have done. She almost had. When he'd told her he'd been living above them, in the ceiling. When he'd told her that and she'd realized it wasn't a joke, she had found herself calculating how quickly she could make it to the bathroom and shut herself in so he couldn't get to her. She had pictured him sneaking around in the dark spaces above them, ear to the floor, listening, probably eventually murdering them all in their sleep. Like something from one of those awful crime dramas her mum watched back-to-back on Sunday nights.

But something about Freddie's manner, the way he stood there, the way he just told her it all...it made her trust him.

After agreeing he would stay for three weeks, she made them each a mug of coffee and told him there needed to be rules. Her mum and dad could have no idea, not even an inkling of an idea, that there was something going on. So, he'd have to carry on exactly as he had been—undetectable. They weren't friends. They weren't going to start having midnight chats through the ceiling, and he absolutely could *not* jump down from the hatch unless she tapped first and told him it was okay. As far as he was concerned, she said, nothing had changed.

After the coffee, she looked at the clock and realized how late it was. She wanted to go to bed. The boy was yawning, so he clearly did too. "Right," she said. "You better show me where you've been sleeping, and then we'll call it a night."

He went first. Walking through the hallway and into her room as if he knew it by heart. He paused by her bed, and they both looked up at the hatch.

"Shall I just...?" he asked.

"Just do what you'd normally do," she replied.

In threadbare socks, he hopped onto the top of her short wooden bookcase and flicked the catch above him. The hatch door dropped into the room, and he reached up. In a swift, practiced maneuver he grabbed hold of the wood around the opening and swung himself up. She heard him turn on the light. The hole flickered, and then harsh attic light flooded out, illuminating her bed. Violet climbed up onto the bookcase and realized she couldn't reach. She took two of her biggest art history hardcovers from the shelf, stacked them on top of each other, and used them as a step.

She didn't follow him into the attic, just stuck her head through the ceiling. He was crouching under the beams. Behind him, amid stacks of shuffled Christmas boxes, was a backpack, a sleeping bag, and a cheap-looking suit hung on a plastic hanger.

"This is it?" she asked. What had she expected?

"Um. Yes." His cheeks flushed, and he looked down at his feet, wiggling an exposed toe.

"Okay," she said. "Well, good night."

"Good night, Violet."

* * *

At 3:00 a.m. Violet was still awake, staring up at the ceiling and straining her ears for the slightest sign of movement. Nothing. Not a creaking floorboard or an accidental sneeze—Freddie was as quiet as a ghost.

She was alone in the house. She should've been freaking out. But all she felt was an overwhelming sense of sadness. Just thinking about being trapped up there made her feel panicky. And he had nothing...nothing to do, nothing to distract himself with. Just a sleeping bag and a backpack. Not even one of those big backpacks people took traveling. A small, school-sized backpack. Was that it? Was his entire life in that bag?

Looking at the stupid air vents her dad had installed when her gran had moved in—and had disconnected as soon as she'd died—she wondered how much Freddie could hear. There was a vent in every room, and he had been living in the attic for six weeks, listening in on her family's dinners and games and arguments. He had probably heard her singing in the mornings. Were the holes in the vents big enough to see through? Probably not.

She knew nothing about him, but she could spot sadness a mile off and Freddie was brimming with it. He wasn't in this situation because he'd done something bad. She was sure of it. And that was why she hadn't asked him how he'd ended up with nowhere to go. And why she would keep his secret.

# 16
## VIOLET

She hadn't slept. She'd spent the night with her brain stuck in a Freddie-Chris-School-Chris-Freddie-School loop. Again, and again her mind taunted her with visions of what might have happened if Freddie hadn't been there. And then she saw herself arriving at school the next morning, everyone already talking about it. And then she saw Freddie. This boy who, actually, now that she thought about it, had risked everything and revealed his secret to help her. She saw him huddled on the street, asking for money, people ignoring him. How many times a week did she walk past someone in a doorway and look at her phone or across the street, so she didn't have to make eye contact with them? One of those people could have been Freddie.

Over and over it all went until, finally, she tired herself out with her own thoughts. When she woke, just two hours later, she was groggy and there was a vicious ache in her temples. She knew he was there, above her, but she still couldn't hear him and, somehow, that made it even stranger.

She should have been going to school. But even as she dressed and packed her books into her bag, she knew she wasn't going. She couldn't. She knew exactly what would happen. She had foolishly reinstated her social media after Aisla had ditched her and had been monitoring it since her alarm went off. There were already memes and photoshopped videos going around.

She had been there less than three weeks, and her reputation was a mess. It was probably totally unsalvageable whether she went in or not. So, when she crossed the street, instead of walking toward the bus stop, she lingered behind a white builder's van and watched her house.

At eight-fifty, Freddie emerged. He was, as he'd told her he would be, wearing a suit. He could have been anybody, just a normal someone on their way to work. She waited until he was out of sight and then let herself back in.

Nothing was out of place. If he'd showered or eaten breakfast, there was no trace of it. In her room, the two hardcovers she'd used last night for a leg up into the attic were still there, so she climbed up and through the hatch. She had to fumble for the light switch, but when she found it, everything was as she remembered it. His sleeping bag and his backpack, one of her gran's old books, and nothing else.

Gingerly, she picked up the backpack. It was depressingly light. She opened it and was about to put her hand inside when something stopped her. This was all he had in the world. She couldn't intrude. She put it back where it was, beside the sleeping bag, and returned to her room.

What kind of awful things must've happened in his life for him to get to this point? For him to get to the point where sleeping in someone else's attic was the best option available? Weren't there charities that helped people like him? And what about his family? Surely, no matter how bad things get, your family's always there for you? Even if she and her mum fell out for a few days, she knew that eventually they would make up. Where was Freddie's family? What about his friends? Yes, things had been rocky since she left Briar Ridge, but she couldn't imagine a world in which she called Aisla and said, "I have nowhere to sleep tonight," and Aisla turned her away.

She wanted to ask Freddie all of these things, of course she did. But she also wanted him to stay, and something told her that if she pried, if she pushed him, he would run. No, Violet would help this boy. She would help him, no questions asked. And the first thing she needed to do was make his sleeping arrangements more bearable.

There was no way she could drag a mattress up into the attic, even if it would fit through the hatch. But she knew precisely where she could find some things to make him more comfortable that wouldn't be missed. Pulling on her knitted mustard-colored cardigan, the one that her mum hated, Violet padded down the hall. She paused opposite her parents' room, but instead of going to their door she turned and went to the one opposite.

As she reached for the handle, she looked down the hallway as if someone might be watching her. Her throat felt tight. Her breath was catching in her chest. She hadn't been in this room since her gran had died. Since the day that Jamie had stopped talking. Since the day it had all started to fall apart.

Violet opened the door. The room was cold, the heating long turned off to save energy or money or whatever the reason. But everything else was exactly as it as it had been. The dresser was still there, with its lacy, white cloth and far too many photo frames housing pictures of Violet and Jamie and their cousins. There was the record player in the corner, the wardrobe that Violet always thought was far too small for someone who had a lifetime's worth of things to keep in it, and the bed with its assortment of cross-stitched cushions.

They had taken away the hospital bed, the wheelchair, and the bed pan not long after her gran had died. Violet was glad they were gone; this was how she remembered her gran's room. This was the place she had come to talk, to laugh, to watch TV shows that she pretended to hate, and to listen to music that she pretended not like. She missed her gran more than anything in the world. And, really, Jamie wasn't the only one who had stopped speaking. The rest of them talked, but about other things. About things that didn't matter. They had mourned together and arranged the funeral together, but after that it was as if her gran had been the one holding everyone together and, without her, a huge gaping chasm opened between them.

If her gran had still been alive, she would've comforted her dad when he had lost his job, she would've spoken words of wisdom, and she would've made him see that he was messing everything up, that he was taking her mum for granted.

Violet shook her head, physically releasing the memories from her brain. This wasn't what she came here for. In the corner of the room, under the window, stood the old, funny-smelling storage heater that her gran had insisted on bringing from her flat. Violet had always quite liked the smell, but her dad had tried again and again to persuade her that she didn't need it. It was on wheels, so Violet dragged it by its cable, down the hall and into her room, then she returned for her gran's blankets—the ones that were folded neatly in a drawer under the bed.

Looking around, she checked for anything else that might have been useful. On the table next to the dresser there was the bowl her gran had used for washing when she could no longer take the twenty-or-so steps to reach the bathroom, some clean flannels, some unused soap. There was also a travel kettle, because she'd still wanted to be able to make her guests a cup of tea, and the mini fridge she'd kept milk and medicines in. Violet took all of it. She was sure that no one would come looking for it, and if they did, she'd simply tell them that she had given it to charity trying to be helpful.

After dragging everything back to her room, she located a spare extension cord in the hall cupboard and squirrelled the items up into the attic. One by one, she pushed her gran's things up through the hatch and then began to spruce up Freddie's sleeping place. She didn't rearrange it completely, that seemed like a step too far, but she neatened up his sleeping bag and tried to make it look more like a bed. She folded a couple of the blankets she'd brought so they looked like pillows, then arranged the kettle and mini fridge on one box and the bowl-come-sink on another.

It took her a while to locate a socket to run the extension cord from, but she knew there was one because the ventilation system had to have been hooked up to something. Once she'd found it, she trailed the cable over the boxes and set up the heater. There was only one thing left to do...

# 17

## FREDDIE

The morning after he met Violet, Freddie didn't know what to do. He listened to her sing along to the radio; heard the opening and closing of wardrobe doors; buried his head in his book when he caught himself wondering whether she was in a towel, skin dimpled with droplets of water, hair wet around her shoulders. And then she left, just like normal. Wondering if it was all some kind of trap, he gingerly opened the hatch and peered down into her room. It was empty. So, he carried on as normal.

It was nearly nine-thirty by the time he reached the town center. Usually, he would linger outside for a few minutes, then when someone who looked like an office worker or businessman went inside, Freddie would join them in the line. He'd pick up a sandwich and a bottle of water, then when he neared the cash register, he'd make a scene of realizing he'd forgotten his wallet. Sometimes the office worker would offer, other times Freddie would have to ask. But, nearly always, they would end up buying his food. Today though, Freddie was on a clock; he needed to focus on cash.

He started at the top of the main street and worked his way down, then up the other side, asking only one person at each coffee shop or ATM. It disturbed him how methodical he'd become and how good at it he was. He knew from looking at a person which line of pretense would work in his favor; he'd even started guessing how much they would give him. He'd quickly stopped asking older people or younger people and focused mainly on those who looked like him—in suits, in a hurry, money in their pockets. Perhaps because he was lucky, perhaps because he'd told Violet he would be gone in three weeks, that day he collected over twenty pounds. And he only felt a little bit bad about it.

Arriving back at the Johnsons' that afternoon, Freddie lingered on the pavement opposite for at least ten minutes, trying to assess whether there were any plain-clothes policemen hiding inside, ready to arrest him. He had spent weeks imagining Violet as the coolest girl on the planet, but even his imagination hadn't stretched this far. He wondered, briefly, whether he was actually still asleep in the attic and dreaming because how was it possible that he'd come out of hiding, told her exactly what he'd been doing all this time, and she'd been totally fine with it?

Satisfied that there didn't seem to be any law enforcement officers lurking in the living room, Freddie stuck to his usual routine and re-entered the Johnsons' bungalow via their back door, returned their key to the jar on the window ledge, peed, washed his face, then approached Violet's door. He pushed it open, climbed up into the attic, and was about to turn on the light when he realized it wasn't actually dark.

Someone—Violet, it had to have been Violet—had strung fairy lights from the beams. He blinked disbelievingly; his lonely sleeping bag had turned into something that actually resembled a bed, with little blanket-pillows and a small box beside it for a table. He brushed his fingers through his hair and tried to force the moisture away from his eyes.

Violet had made him a home.

# 18
## FREDDIE

Violet had made it clear they were *not* friends. But after what she did for him, Freddie needed to find a way to say thank you. So the next day, after the lunchtime rush had died down, he took his earnings and went to the second-hand bookshop. The door jingled as he entered, and the second it closed behind him, he was transported by the smell. His mum had owned an entire library's worth of second-hand books. She'd collected them—but not for their value. She had chosen books with intriguing inscriptions or beautiful covers, and she had always invented fantastical stories about their history. His favorite had been a copy of *The Great Gatsby*. The inscription had read,

*For Harold. A thank you for a wonderful summer.*
*How very decadent we were.*

*Love always, Eleanor.*
*02.09.77*

Freddie's mum had crafted a long and elaborate scenario in which Harold and Eleanor had been students at the University of Oxford. Harold had been wildly wealthy, and Eleanor had been there on a scholarship. They had been from two different worlds, but they'd hit it off and fallen head over heels in love. Upon graduating, Harold had whisked Eleanor away to a villa in Italy, where they had spent the summer drinking wine from his vineyard and sailing on his yacht. They had lived to excess, indulging themselves utterly because they knew that when those heady days were over, they would return home and they would go their separate ways, unable to reconcile the paths carved out for them.

When Janet had boxed up his mum's books, Freddie had tried to sneak Harold and Eleanor's volume away, but Janet had found it, tossed it in with the rest, and given them to an auction house to either sell or ditch.

Freddie forced himself to move from the doormat. He still felt awkward whenever he approached someone in a shop or café, and he expected the manager to narrow his eyes and step back slightly. However, when Freddie cleared his throat and asked whether they had any books about pen-and-ink drawing, the man smiled and said, "Of course, sir."

The art history books were on the first floor at the top of a spiral staircase at the back of the shop. It wasn't a particularly large selection, and the man rubbed his chin and hmmed while he looked for something that might fit Freddie's brief. "I don't think we have anything about pen and ink specifically. How about this?" He handed Freddie a not-too-thick volume entitled *Drawing for Children: Illustrating in Ink.*

Freddie opened the book. There was no inscription. Perfect. He could write his own.

# 19
## VIOLET

In the one day that Violet had been absent from school, Chris Parker had told everyone about Wednesday night. Except, of course, he had been rather economical with the truth. In Chris's version, Violet had invited him over, gotten drunk after just two glasses of wine, stripped naked, lap danced, and vomited. Her absence had merely added proof to the theory that she was hungover and mortified and hiding. She should have been braver. She should have gone in and told them all what really happened, maybe even asked Freddie to go with her and back her up.

Jeanette Simmons was the first to speak to her. A plump, greasy-looking girl who always had cat hair on her mismatched, oversized clothes. Violet was standing stock still, unable to make herself step over the threshold when Jeanette tapped her shoulder. "It'll die down. By lunchtime they'll be talking about something else."

It was something a teacher would say or a mum or an aunt. But it was enough to get Violet moving. She allowed Jeanette to shield her as they headed toward their lockers. "We've never spoken. How come you're being so nice?"

Jeanette shrugged. "I'm a nice person, I guess."

Violet nodded. "What he's saying—it's not true. I mean, he came over, but that's not what happened."

"He's an idiot."

* * *

At lunch, Violet walked through the cafeteria with her head down, trying not to make eye contact with anyone. The only empty table was the round one near the garbage bins. She'd been prodding at her sandwich and stirring her vending machine hot chocolate for at least five minutes when someone said, "Can I sit?"

Jeanette put her tray down before Violet had chance to say anything and tucked a napkin into the collar of her blouse. The blouse had flamingos on it, and the buttons across her stomach looked in danger of popping.

"Thanks. Again," said Violet.

"No problem," Jeanette said, mouth full of baked potato, mayonnaise dripping onto her chin. She ate as if food was about to be outlawed. Violet tried not to look.

Although she was grateful for Jeanette's company, she was also aware that the events of the past week were forming the building blocks for the rest of her time at Arnhurst and that if Jeanette became her friend or even her acquaintance...well, that was it. She was finished.

But maybe she was finished already.

She and Jeanette ate lunch in relative silence. They had math together, so they talked about Mr. Jenkins for a bit and about the weird substitute teacher they'd had this morning who looked like a cartoon hippo. But then Jeanette had taken out her phone and stopped talking and, in the end, Violet had gone to the art room to sketch.

By the time she got home, she was well and truly ready to shut herself away and drown out the world. Something with a heavy beat and lots of violins would do it. She had thought of Freddie only briefly, and his presence was so undetectable she almost wondered whether he had left.

She put her bag on her desk and unclipped her hair from its ponytail, then saw something she didn't recognize. A book. On her bed. *Drawing for Children: Illustrating in Ink.* This was not one of her books. It looked old—it smelled old. She sniffed it as she opened it. Usually, she hated people writing in books. But somehow, this time, she didn't seem to mind. On the inside cover was the message,

*For Violet*
*One good turn...*
*F*

# 20
## FREDDIE

For two weeks after their first meeting, Freddie didn't see or hear anything from Violet, and he was keenly aware that his deadline was approaching. He'd saved what he had set out to save. Had almost enough for two months' rent. He should've been excited, buzzing at the prospect of leaving his confines and starting his new life—finally becoming Freddie 2.0. But...he wasn't.

He had gathered that Violet was having a tough time at school because her music was shouty and loud, and there was a lot of door slamming and stomping about. After he left her the drawing book, he'd expected—or hoped for—a note saying thank you, but nothing had appeared. Then one day, he returned to find a hardcover book with a postcard on top of it. On the reverse of the postcard, Violet had written simply,

*Let me know what you think.*

Freddie could barely contain his grin. He couldn't remember the last time he'd smiled like that—so hard it almost ached. In the attic, he turned on the fairy lights, took off his suit, hung it back up, got into his jeans and his hoodie, made a cup of tea with the miniature kettle Violet had given him, and sat cross-legged on his bed. He placed his fingers on the book's cover and traced the words: *Hope is the Thing with Feathers: The Complete Poems of Emily Dickinson.*

He'd heard of Emily Dickinson. He had a vague feeling that she was American and that she'd died a long time ago, but he'd never read any of her poetry. He opened it, fighting the urge to plow through as quickly as possible so he could tell Violet he'd finished. She'd asked him to let her know what he thought, which meant he needed to actually have some thoughts worth thinking.

At first, he read as if he was trying to decipher an unknown exam text, jotting notes in the back of the Navy SEAL book. But then he stopped making notes and just read the words, and it was like getting into a warm bath when you ache all over. He read until it was late and the Johnsons were all asleep. Then, the next morning, he borrowed a Post-it note from Violet's desk and wrote,

*I didn't want it to stop. Can I keep it a while?*
*I'd like to read them all again.*

\* \* \*

That afternoon, he'd only just sealed himself back in the attic when he heard the front door open half an hour ahead of schedule. The clatter of boots against the shoe rack told him it was Ellie. She was never usually home this early. Violet was always first.

Freddie listened as Ellie walked from the hall to the kitchen and flipped on the kettle. He imagined the soft suck of the fridge door as it opened and pictured her reaching inside for the milk. He was about to return to his bed when the doorbell rang.

Ellie greeted the visitor with a worn out, "Hi," but Freddie couldn't work out the visitor's reply.

The closing of the double doors that led from the hall to the living room indicated that Ellie and her visitor were moving through to the kitchen.

"Coffee?" Ellie asked.

"Please," a female replied. Then, "How are you doing, El?"

"Oh, H. I don't know. It's just getting harder. I thought he'd have grown out of it by now, I really did."

"I'm sure he will. How long has it been now?" "H" spoke in a voice that reminded Freddie of the nose plugs his mum used to make him wear for swimming lessons.

"Nearly a year."

"And what does his therapist say?"

"Don't pressure him, let him work through it, just try to behave normally. But, H. How can I? It's not normal, is it?" Ellie's words were thickening as though they were too big for her mouth. Was she crying?

"Kids find all sorts of ways to deal with grief. I'm sure Jamie's just using it as a coping mechanism. It's like... having an imaginary friend. Just be patient."

Jamie. They were talking about Jamie. Freddie had figured out quite quickly that *ST* on the Johnsons' calendar stood for *speech therapist* and that the appointments were for Jamie because he never spoke. Never. In the beginning, Freddie had thought maybe his voice was just too small for him to hear, but then he'd realized there was no laughter, no screaming. Kids Jamie's age screamed all the time. Happy screams, sad screams. Amy had squealed at just about anything.

Ellie sighed. "It should have been one of us who found her. Pete said from the beginning it wasn't a good idea."

"Listen, you were doing the best you could. No one can blame you for that. Losing a grandparent is hard for any kid. Jamie's just dealing with it in his own special way. What does the school say?"

"They've been great. Really supportive. I just worry."

Freddie imagined H reaching out and squeezing Ellie's hand. "'Course you do."

"Thanks for coming over; it's good to talk to someone who's a bit more...impartial. Pete and I just end up arguing."

"You never need to thank me, silly." H's voice was softer now. "What about—this might sound strange—but what about a pet? You know, something he can be responsible for. Interact with. No pressure?"

Ellie laughed. "Pete would never have it. He's not an animal person."

"Shame. I've seen heaps of stuff on TV lately—they use dogs in schools now to help children read. All sorts."

"Pete would never say yes. It's silly, really, because I think he'd enjoy it if I just brought an animal home. I think he'd see the benefits. It's just getting it past the front door!"

\* \* \*

Violet didn't play much music after dinner, so he went to sleep earlier than normal. He must have been in a deep sleep because it took him a while to register that something was happening.

*TAP. TAPTAPTAP.*

Someone was knocking on the hatch door. It was opening. Christ.

He shuffled backward on his blanket and fumbled for the switch that would turn off the fairy lights, but it was too late. A head emerged from below.

"Violet?"

"You busy?"

"What time is it?"

"Eleven. Why?"

He felt disorientated. "I was asleep."

"Oh, sorry." She started to duck back down. "Of course, you were."

"Wait, it's okay." He crawled toward her, whispering. "Is everyone in bed?"

"Hours ago."

"Is everything okay? I thought you weren't supposed to talk to me?"

Violet laughed a little, then held out her hand. He helped her up, and she sat down at the bottom of his bed, leaning against a box. "I didn't expect you to like it."

He must have been frowning because she gestured to the book she'd lent him. It was on his sleeping bag. He'd read himself to sleep. "You didn't?"

"Most guys think it's lame."

"I don't."

She paused, smiling. "Okay, well. You're welcome to keep it for a bit."

"Thanks. I can lend you *At Home with the Navy SEAL* in return?"

Violet laughed, then put her hand over her mouth. "Sorry, too loud. Um. No, you're all right, thanks. I'll leave that one with you."

"If you're sure. It's a real page-turner."

Violet shook her head. Her hair fell forward, and she tucked it back behind her ear. "So, how's it going? The plan?"

Freddie looked at his bag, where his money was stashed. He now had almost three hundred pounds. "Good. I just need to start looking for a room to rent."

Violet shrugged as if it didn't matter. Had she forgotten she said three weeks? "It's weird. I never hear you. Sometimes I wonder if you've left. You're good at being invisible."

Freddie laughed.

"Did I say something funny?"

He leaned forward and rested his elbows on his knees. "Not funny. Ironic, maybe. Being homeless, that's kind of what you become: invisible. In a way, that's the worst thing about it. For me, anyway." He stopped, unsure whether she wanted to hear any more.

Violet cleared her throat and looked down at a hole in her jeans. It seemed to be a deliberate hole. A fashionable hole. "How do you mean?"

Freddie uncrossed his legs. "It's like...you stop existing. People don't see you. Or if they do, they pretend not to because they're uncomfortable."

"I've done that," she said in a small voice.

"So have I. Before..." He stopped. He didn't want to talk about before, so he offered her a cereal bar and said,

"There are four kinds of people—the ones who genuinely care and ask what they can do to help, and there are the ones who help you to make themselves feel better. Like this guy who was clearly on a first date and went into McDonald's specifically to buy me a Big Mac. He presented it to me in front of the girl he was with, and they weren't even out of earshot before he said, 'You know I'm a vegetarian and I wouldn't normally even go *near* the place, but the poor guy, he'll live off that for a week.'"

Violet laughed as Freddie put on a posh accent but said, "That's awful!"

He nodded. "Right? But then there are the ones who don't know what to do, so they pretend they haven't seen you or look at their phone or cross the street. Those people, I get. Like I said, I was one of them." He looked away from her, at the fairy lights. "But the ones that hurt are the ones who literally don't see you at all. They're oblivious. You don't even register as a blip in their peripheral vision. And that's most people. To most people, you're not even human anymore." It was the most he'd spoken in so long that he felt a little breathless.

Violet shook her head, and as she breathed out, her nostrils flared. Suddenly, Freddie felt as if he'd said too much. She looked on the verge of asking him something, and he didn't want to lie to her but there were things he couldn't say.

"How long were you..."

This was it. The lead-up had begun. "Eighteen months," he said. A short answer. Not an invite to ask more.

Violet studied him for a second. She hadn't opened her cereal bar and was rubbing the end of the wrapper between her thumb and forefinger. She handed it back to him. Then she looked at her phone. "I better go."

Freddie smiled. "'Course." And, as she ducked back down into her room, "Violet?"

She popped her head back up. "Yeah?"

"I thought you said no midnight chats?"

She smiled up at him. "Mm. But if you're going to stay a bit longer, we might as well get to know each other."

"Longer?"

"Can't chuck you out before Christmas, can I? Besides, you'll need a while to find a place. Better to start in the new year."

"You're sure?"

"Well, let's see what you think of the next book I bring you, and then we'll decide, huh?"

Freddie was certain she winked at him as she closed the hatch.

# DECEMBER

DECEMBER

# 21

## FREDDIE

On the first of December, the world spiraled into a Christmas-induced stupor. Town became hectic, splashed with lights, music, giant blow-up snowmen, and people dressed as Santa or elves or reindeer. Everyone was in a hurry. Barely anyone had time to stop, and Freddie's takings had slowed to no more than six or seven pounds a day. Funny, really, that Christmas spirit seemed to be working in reverse.

He tried not to think about how much he hated what he was doing. He tried to see it as just a means to an end. Okay, it wasn't good. But once he was back on his feet he'd donate to charity or volunteer or do something to redeem himself.

Apart from the guilt that gnawed away at his stomach, Freddie had another problem: he was beginning to bump into the same people. People who'd already helped him once and would, surely, be suspicious if he pleaded poverty a second time. He had a good memory for faces so he usually managed to avoid the ones he'd approached before, but it was becoming more and more difficult. Still, after Christmas he'd be stopping. He'd be finding a room and a job and saying goodbye to his daily untruths.

For now, though, he decided to try the "rougher" end of town. He positioned himself next to an ATM, planning on waiting until someone approached and then fumble in his pockets and mutter, "Please, not today, please..." But then he looked up and saw Pete Johnson.

Pete was walking toward him. Big, confident strides. Straight toward him. Freddie panicked. He could feel the heat rising from his throat to his cheeks. But Pete didn't even notice him. He just punched in his PIN and withdrew a stack of twenty-pound notes. There must have been at least three hundred pounds.

Pete pocketed the money quickly and crossed the street. He lingered for a moment, looked at his watch, then smiled. Approaching him, a blonde woman in a red coat and matching lipstick smiled back. They stepped in line with each other, walking side by side toward the only marked building on the street: a seedy, dark, not-the-kind-of-place-you'd-go-for-a-business-meeting hotel called the Ellington.

For a long time, Freddie didn't move. He felt like he'd just found out that Santa Claus wasn't real. He knew the Johnsons weren't perfect. But he believed that Ellie and Pete were solid. Unshakable. Every Friday since their spontaneous night away, Pete had organized a date night. He'd even been coming home earlier some evenings. Surely, he wasn't seeing someone else. Why would he? Why would he risk everything?

Freddie was aware that he was making assumptions. But whatever was going on, he was pretty sure Pete wasn't telling Ellie about it. Maybe Freddie should find a way to tell her? Or maybe he should tell Violet? No. He couldn't. Not before Christmas.

As he decided this, he couldn't quite figure out whether it was for the Johnsons' benefit or for his own; even if he was only going to be listening to their Christmas dinner, at least he would be close, and he wanted— needed—it to be a good one.

Last Christmas, Freddie's first without a home to go to, had been awful. He'd started walking on Christmas Eve and walked right through the night, reaching his old town at 11:00 a.m. on Christmas morning. It had taken a further hour to reach his house. Not the place they'd lost to the repo agents—the home he'd grown up in. The place that held memories of his mum and Amy and happiness.

By the time he'd gotten there his feet had been bleeding and he'd been shaking with tiredness. The sloping driveway that led up to the garage and the front door had given him chills. But still, he'd stared at them for a long time. Eventually, he'd sat down in front of a lamppost and leaned back against it. It had been unseasonably warm for December, and the sun had been shining but, somehow, that had made him feel worse. He'd wanted rain. And cold. And stinging stripes of hail that would lash at his face and make him sorry.

By four-thirty it had gotten dark, and Freddie had done what he'd been planning to do since he'd started his journey the day before. He'd crept up the grassy bank to the left of the drive and walked up to the front door. On either side of the door there was a glass panel. His mum had always talked about getting blinds for them, but she'd never gotten around to it, and when his dad had mentioned it to Janet, she'd dismissed the idea immediately. She'd liked people to be able to see in.

The new family hadn't had blinds either, and Freddie had pressed himself up as close as he could to the glass. There had been no voice in his head telling him not to and no fear of being caught. He'd just needed to see.

His old house was open plan. In front of him, the dining table had been strewn with Christmas cracker remnants and dirty plates. A partly devoured box of chocolates had been in the center. He'd licked his lips. To the right, the living room. Two women in their thirties had been hugging. Twins, boys, about ten, had been crashing a remote-controlled drone into the ceiling. An elderly couple had been asleep in the corner, and a dog had been barking at the drone. A man had entered from the kitchen and started clearing the plates. He'd glanced toward the door. Freddie hadn't moved. The man had squinted. "Hey, Anna, I think someone's at your..."

Freddie backed away.

"Hey!"

He'd run. Down the drive, across the street, back the way he'd come. The man had begun running after him.

"Hey! You!"

Freddie's heart had been pounding. His mouth had gone dry. His feet had hurt so much they'd almost stopped hurting. The man hadn't caught him, and by the time he'd walked back to Newton, Christmas had ended.

This year would be better, but it wouldn't be easy;

with the Johnsons home from work and school for the holidays, there was every chance he'd be stuck in the attic for a week or more—unable to climb down and breathe fresh air or gather food or wash. The thought of it made him feel itchy and nervous. He could go to the Pay What You Can Kitchen and see Gina, but he could only go there if he could get in and out.

He needed to talk to Violet about it, but he hadn't finished the next book she'd brought him and didn't know whether making contact about something un-book-related would've been crossing some kind of boundary. The problem, however, was solved for him when, around ten-thirty that night Violet tapped on the hatch.

"We have a problem," she said as she climbed up into his space.

Freddie looked down into her room.

"They're out. But tomorrow is Christmas decorations day, which means..."

Freddie glanced back at the boxes surrounding his sleeping area. "The boxes?"

"Yep. Lucky for you, Dad's working tomorrow, and Mum can't get up here 'cause of her foot so I said I'd pass the stuff down to her. But you're going to have to be *super ghostly* quiet when we do it."

Freddie felt a bit sick. What if Pete didn't go to work? If he even was working. It was Saturday tomorrow, after all. What if he had an attack of conscience and decided to stay home and help his wife decorate the house? Freddie tried to say, "Okay," but it came out as a croaky meaningless sound.

Violet touched his arm. "It'll be fine."

"Mm-hmm."

* * *

The next morning, Violet started playing the Mariah Carey Christmas song that Freddie hated, and he knew this was his cue to scurry as far away from the hatch as possible. He'd spent the early hours of the morning quietly packing away his things and rearranging the items Violet brought him so it looked like they'd simply been left up here by Ellie or Pete along with everything else. And then he'd waited.

Violet played the song on repeat, and when it stopped Freddie knew this was the moment. The hatch swung open, and Ellie's voice drifted up. "Be careful, Vi. Your dad should be doing this."

"Mum, we do it every year. Dad's never around. And he hates Christmas."

"He doesn't *hate* Christmas. It was just never really a thing for him growing up. His parents didn't make a big deal of it."

"But Grandma loved Christmas!" Violet's head emerged through the hole, and she pressed her index finger to her lips. Freddie nodded and stayed, cross-legged, in his corner.

"She did when you and Jamie came along, but she was never that... What's the word? Friendly. With your father. Growing up."

Violet was dragging boxes toward the hatch, and Freddie wished he could help. He tried to pick out all the ones that said *XMAS* on them, but Violet couldn't make it look too easy, so she gestured for him to stop.

She started passing them down. "Why don't you ever say anything nice about her?" Her tone had sharpened.

Ellie took a moment to respond. "Sorry, Vi. I just had a very different relationship with her, I suppose. I didn't see the same side of her that you did."

"Well, I miss her. And I think we should talk about her more. It might help Jay if we—"

"Violet," Ellie dropped one of the boxes onto the floor of Violet's room with a thump. "Now isn't the time for this conversation."

"There's never a time," Violet muttered, more to Freddie or the empty space in between them than to her mother.

Ellie changed the subject and started asking Violet whether she wanted turkey, goose, or one of those three-in-one birds they do now for Christmas dinner. Soon, all that was left was the Christmas tree.

"Vi, are you sure you can manage? If not, we can wait until Dad—"

Violet sent the Christmas tree box hurtling onto the bed, then peered down and said, "Yep. Managed it."

# 22

## VIOLET

After putting up the decorations, Violet and Jamie headed out for the evening. He loved it when it was just the two of them, but she was struggling to mirror his level of enthusiasm. They were going to the Arnhurst Christmas concert. Jeanette was in it, of course she was, and she'd invited Violet to go and see her perform. It was exactly the opposite of anything Violet considered fun, but, somehow, she and Jeanette had become friends and she felt as if she owed her.

Chris and his followers were still taunting her but it was clear they were losing interest, and having Jeanette was better than having no one. She was even kind of funny. Sometimes. So, Violet had agreed to go and had decided to take Jamie with her. Their mum thought it was a lovely idea, and Violet could see her mentally cataloging how many hours she would have to herself in an empty house to just "be"—that's what she always said—"You know, Pete. I would like, just once, to have some time to just 'be'. Just sit. Not to read or watch TV or vacuum or work or look after the kids. Just...be."

Except their mum wouldn't be alone. Freddie would be up there in the ceiling, and their mum would have absolutely no idea. Sometimes, in moments like these, it dawned on Violet just how creepy the entire situation was. If their mum knew, she would be so freaked out she'd probably want to move to a new house. Their dad wouldn't be freaked, he'd be angry. But they didn't know Freddie was there, and Violet intended to keep it that way.

\* \* \*

The concert was dismal, as anticipated. But Jeanette ran up to them afterward and gave Violet an enormous, sweaty hug. "Thanks so much for coming!"

"Well, I said I would. This is Jamie, my little brother."

Jeanette hugged Jamie too, and he wrinkled his nose as he came a little too close to her armpits.

"Is your family here?" Violet asked, wondering what Mr. and Mrs. Jeanette were like.

Jeanette looked momentarily unsure but then said, "Oh no, they're coming tomorrow."

Violet nodded. "Cool. Okay well, good luck for the rest of the shows. See you Monday?"

"Yep, yes. I mean, see you." Jeanette was blushing.

As they walked away, Jamie squeezed Violet's hand, and when she looked at him, he rolled his eyes in such a grown up, almost mum, kind of way that she guffawed with laughter. She tousled his hair and pulled him close. She knew she should be nicer to him. He was such a good boy, really. "Love you, dude."

Jamie didn't say it back. But he stopped, tugged her down to his level, and kissed her cheek.

* * *

On Monday morning, Jeanette was full of herself. She was bouncy and smiley. Violet had never seen her so happy.

"You really like performing, don't you?" Violet asked her as they walked toward their impending math lesson.

"Don't you?"

Violet shook her head and shuddered. "No. Definitely not."

Jeanette did a twirl in the middle of the hallway. Sometimes, it was as if she actually wanted people to think she was strange. "But it's the chance to be someone else. Anyone else. You put on a mask and pretend you're someone who's confident and good at stuff and..." she stopped, noticing Violet frowning at her.

"Why not just be you?"

Jeanette laughed. "Have you met me?"

Violet rolled her eyes. "Jeanette. You don't need to be someone else. You just do you, and eventually someone will get you. When we're free of this place." Violet looked up at the ceiling as if there might be an escape route she hadn't noticed.

Jeanette looped her arm through Violet's and squeezed. "That's why I'm glad you came here, Violet. You're not like the others."

Violet sighed. There was no point fighting it. Jeanette was her friend. And she was actually beginning to like her.

They rounded the corner, still arm in arm. They were late, and the hallway was deserted. Jeanette was midway through a rendition of "I Dreamed a Dream", and Violet was telling her to be quiet or someone would come and tell them off for not being in class when, seemingly out of nowhere, Chris Parker and the girls from the back of the bus appeared in front of them. Chris was holding something—a bucket. So were the girls. Violet pulled Jeanette's arm, tried to get her to turn around, but it was too late.

Whatever was in the buckets, it reeked. The smell made Violet want to be instantly and horrendously sick. Jeanette was screaming. Chris didn't say anything, but as he walked away, he looked Violet up and down as if he wished she was dead, and she was pretty sure one of the girls spat at her. Violet turned to Jeanette. "I'm so sorry. This is my fault." But Jeanette pushed her away and ran.

A few minutes later, Violet was discovered, still in the same spot, by Mr. Jenkins. "Ah," he said nervously, probably worried he was about to end up with a crying teenage girl covered in God-knows-what in his office. "I'll, ah, I'll get Miss Perkins."

Miss Perkins helped Violet wash the worst of it from her hands and face. "I think it's food," she said, picking something out of Violet's hair.

That was when Violet started to cry.

Miss Perkins patted her on the shoulder and shook her head. "I'm sorry you're having a bad time here, Violet. This isn't the kind of school we want to be. If you tell me who did this to you, I can help."

"How?"

Miss Perkins sighed. "You know we have CCTV in the hallways?"

"Then why do you need me to tell you?" Violet stopped crying and stormed out. She knew what would happen next—they'd talk to her parents, Chris's parents. They'd put them all in a room, and it would change precisely nothing, except that it would make her mum and dad feel horribly guilty for moving her from Briar Ridge and start a whole new round of arguments.

Exiting the school gates, she took out her phone and texted Aisla. *Need to see you. Life is awful. Miss you. Please text me back.* She sounded pathetic and needy, but she didn't care.

Instead of going to the bus stop, and despite the fact she smelled terrible and should have gone home to shower, Violet found herself walking into town. As she reached the main street, the cheerfulness of it all made her feel worse. And when a woman dressed as Mrs. Claus, with red-and-white-striped tights and a too-short velvet dress, thrust a bucket toward her, asking for donations for the children's center Christmas party, Violet panicked, shoving it into Mrs. Claus's chest and ran.

She was aiming for Starbucks. When Freddie first told her about his routine, he'd said that was one of the places he "worked", and she didn't know why but, right now, he was the only person she could think of who might understand how she was feeling.

She saw him before he saw her, walking out of Starbucks in his suit, chatting to a girl in her twenties with dark brown hair and dazzling blue eyes. She was laughing at something he was saying, and for a moment Violet felt horribly jealous. But then she heard Freddie saying, "Thanks ever so much, Lucy."

"No problem. I remember being an intern—what a nightmare! Hope you find the company card soon."

Freddie rolled his eyes. "Me too!" He was waving goodbye to Lucy with the dazzling eyes when Violet tapped him on the shoulder. His grinned. "Violet, what..." Then he noticed the smell. His nose wrinkled as he took in her appearance. "What happened?"

She was out of breath from running, her cheeks were red, and she was on the verge of crying again. The street was too busy. People were looking at her strangely. "Can we go somewhere?"

Freddie nodded. "Of course."

He took her to the kind of café her mum wouldn't have been seen dead inside. From the street, it looked dirty. The walls were purple, but the paint was peeling, a poster on the side of the building had been reposted so many times it was no longer clear what it was supposed to be, and the sign was hanging off. But inside, it was quiet and there were booths with worn leather seats and plastic checked tablecloths. Violet slid into one and looked around. It was surprisingly cozy, and a blackboard behind the till said that coffee was only 50p on Mondays, with unlimited refills.

Placing a mug and a doughnut in front of her, Freddie said, "Sugar always helps." She smiled and sipped at the coffee. Actually it wasn't bad. He was waiting for her to speak.

Violet sighed. "Remember the guy you saved me from?"

"You mean the really huge guy I bravely stood up to?"

"That's the one."

"He did this?" Freddie was looking at her mulch-sodden clothes.

Violet nodded. "I thought he was over it but turns out he was just lulling me into a false sense of security."

Something she hadn't seen before flashed across Freddie's face. "Want me to—"

"What? Deal with him?"

"If you need me to."

"No, no it's fine." She sighed. "I just need to not let it bother me. He'll get bored."

Freddie raised an eyebrow as if to say, Will he? And when she didn't respond he asked, "Were you looking for me?"

She looked down into her coffee, and when she looked up, he was smiling.

"Eat your doughnut," he said, taking an enormous bite of his and letting a sugary mustache form on his upper lip. "Competition—first to lick their lips buys the next coffee."

"It says unlimited refills."

"Okay, first to lick their lips is a massive loser until the end of time."

Violet laughed, and when he licked his lips first, she was pretty sure he did it deliberately.

# 23

## FREDDIE

With just a week to go until Christmas, Freddie was still trying to decide what to get Violet as a gift. They hadn't spoken since the doughnut, but she'd continued to leave him books, one a week, each with a different postcard and a different message.

The drawing book that had started their mini secret book club had been a stroke of inspiration, but now, he needed to get Violet a Christmas present and he couldn't think of anything within his budget that would say what he needed it to say. What could he possibly buy that would convey *you saved my life*?

He was wandering through the town's Christmas market, which had been surprisingly profitable for him over the last few days, when he saw a stall selling handmade wooden trinkets: keyrings, toy trains, plaques with inspirational quotes on them. Freddie used to be good at woodwork. He'd always enjoyed it, but his dad had told him not to be so silly—no one was a carpenter these days. These days, kids studied business or computer science and made tons of money so they could care for their parents in their old age.

Freddie picked up one of the toy trains and weighed it up and down in his palm. He turned it over, looking at the smoothness of the wood, the way the grain told a story, told you its history.

"For a friend?" the clerk interrupted him.

Freddie looked up and smiled, handing back the train. "Oh, no, I just... How did you get to do this?"

The man frowned. "What do you mean, son?"

"I mean, um, how do you do this as a job?"

The man laughed. "Well, *job* implies it makes me a living. It's more of a hobby, but I'm a carpenter by trade. You know—kitchens, doors, garden gates, that sort of thing."

Freddie could feel his eyes brightening. "Is that an easy job to get? Being a carpenter? Are there exams?"

The man folded his arms. "Not easy, but not difficult if you've got a knack for it. These days you'd need an apprenticeship. A couple of days a week at trade school and a couple of days on the job getting paid."

"Paid?"

"Mm." The man narrowed his eyes and glanced at Freddie's hands. "You, ah, done anything like this before?"

Freddie shrugged. "I used to. I enjoyed it at school, but my dad wanted me to do business so..."

"And what do you do now?"

"Nothing really. I'm trying to decide—"

The man scratched his chin. "All right, I tell you what.

Here's my business card. And here's"—he reached into the apron that was slung around his middle—"a crappy old piece of wood. You turn that into something beautiful, give me a call, and I'll hook you up with a friend of mine who's looking for a new apprentice."

Freddie didn't know what to say. He gripped the piece of wood as if it was a bag of diamonds. "Really?"

"Mm-hmm."

"Thank you."

"Merry Christmas, son."

Freddie knew exactly what he was going to make. He was going to make Violet a Christmas present, and it was going to be the most beautiful thing she'd ever owned. At the next stall, he purchased a gift bag and some tissue paper with penguins on it. Then, because it was Christmas and he felt he deserved it, and because it was getting colder and colder as the days wore on, he bought himself a coat. Not a second-hand coat. A new coat. Only fifteen pounds and not particularly fashionable, but new.

As he walked back toward the bus stop with his Christmas shopping in his hand, money in his wallet, the glimmer of a job, and his brand-new coat, he felt almost normal. This was what his new life would be like—freedom, independence, Violet?

Just before the bus stop, he passed the window of the toy shop. He thought he should get something for Jamie too. He went inside and was looking at a display of dog puppets when a voice made him stop and turn so suddenly that a woman with a stroller careered into the back of him and yelled, "Seriously?!"

"Amy?" Freddie pushed past the stroller and, almost

running, grinning from ear to ear, grabbed hold of the
girl whose voice he'd heard. She had dark hair, a little
pink hat, and big brown eyes. "Amy?" His hand was
gripping her arm.

The girl looked terrified.

Someone wrenched Freddie's hand away and said,
"What the hell are you doing?"

The girl was not Amy. Of course, she wasn't. "I'm so
sorry. I thought she was someone else. I'm sorry."

\* \* \*

That night, he had a nightmare. The first in a long time.
And it was a bad one. So bad that Violet didn't even tap
when she opened the hatch, she just jumped through
the opening and whispered, "What the hell's going on?"

Freddie was crouched on his bed, arms around his
knees. It was pitch black.

"Freddie? Are you okay? What's happening?"

He tried to speak, but nothing came out.

Violet fumbled for the fairy lights and turned them on.
He was sweating, and she must have been able to see
it because she crawled forward very slowly, like he was
a stray dog in a cage, and said, "It's okay."

"Did I shout?"

"No, just lots of thrashing."

"Do you think your parents heard?"

Violet shook her head as if he shouldn't worry about
it. "I'll tell them it's pigeons or something. Really big
pigeons." She was trying to make him smile. "Mutant
pigeons..."

He tried but couldn't.

"Was it a nightmare?" She opened the mini fridge and passed him a bottle of water.

He nodded.

"Want to talk about it?"

He shook his head.

Violet held out her hand for the bottle and took a swig of his water. He found it oddly intimate and looked away. She was wearing lemon-colored pajamas. The top was long sleeved, but she looked cold. He handed her a blanket. She wrapped it around her shoulders and said, "I used to have them. I'd scream and everything."

"Really?" He was glad she was talking.

"Yeah. After my gran died. That's when Jamie stopped speaking."

"You were close to her?"

Violet sighed. "She lived here. Jamie ran in there every day after school. The day she died he'd done her this painting of a giraffe 'cause that was her favorite animal. It didn't look anything like a giraffe, but..." She stopped and looked down at her nails. They were a minty green color but chipped at the edges. "Sorry. I'm making this about me."

"No, it's okay. Please..." Freddie wanted it to be about her. Wanted to just sit there and listen and stop the images in his brain.

"It's supposed to not be as bad if someone's old when they die. People ask, 'How old was she?' as if the fact she was eighty makes it okay. Like, oh well, she had a good life. Never mind."

Freddie nodded. He didn't remember his grandparents, but even when his mum had died people said things like, *Oh, but she had a wonderful life.*

Violet looked at him and spoke as if she genuinely wanted him to answer her. "But if you love someone—it doesn't matter, does it? If they lived eighty years or fifty or twelve. It doesn't stop you missing them. Does it?"

"No. It doesn't," he said.

"I miss her. She was my friend. You know? But no one talks about her. Not just Jamie—Mum, Dad... It's the anniversary tomorrow. One year. I asked Dad if he was going to take flowers to the grave, but he said he's working, and graves are just symbolic. They don't mean anything." Her voice was becoming wobbly, and she pushed her glasses up her nose and blinked hard.

Freddie leaned forward a little. "I could go with you. If you..."

"Would you?"

"Of course."

She smiled and wrinkled her nose. "Okay. Yes. Thank you. It's the cemetery on Bridge Street."

"I'll meet you after school."

"How come I was supposed to be helping you with your problem and now you're helping me with mine?"

Freddie wanted to reach out and take her hand, but instead he just smiled and said, "Trust me, you are helping me, Violet."

\* \* \*

The next day, he was waiting at the gates of the cemetery at three-thirty. At three-forty-five he saw Violet's pale hair and bright red coat in the distance. But she wasn't alone. She had brought Jamie. His heart started fluttering. He wondered whether to jump behind the wall, but Violet waved a mittened hand at him and then leaned down and said something to Jamie. Jamie waved too.

She was carrying a bunch of flowers and smiled as she approached him. "Freddie. This is Jamie."

Jamie waved again.

Freddie extended his hand, and Jamie grinned as he shook it. "Pleased to meet you, Jamie."

As they entered the gates, Violet gave Jamie the flowers and he ran ahead. "You don't mind, do you?" she asked, turning to him and putting her hand on his forearm.

"Of course not."

"I told him you're a friend."

Freddie looked at her out of the corner of his eye. "A friend?"

"Yes."

At the grave, Violet didn't cry. She helped Jamie lay out the flowers, and she said, "We miss you, Grandma. We miss how you always made us a drink when we got in from school with your little travel kettle, even when you weren't feeling very well. And we miss watching silly old musicals with you, and Kit Kats on Sundays. And even if we don't say it out loud, we miss you all the time."

As they left, Violet asked her brother if he was glad they came, and he nodded and nuzzled her arm. "Me too," she said. "Me too."

On the bus back home, the three of them sat in the back seat, and when Freddie asked Jamie how old he was he held up six pudgy, gloved fingers. Freddie made himself smile. "Whoa. Six?! What an awesome age. And what's your favorite thing? Dinosaurs? Dragons?"

"He likes pugs. Obsessed," Violet answered for her brother.

"Pugs? Are they the ones with the faces like this..." Freddie squished his nose and crossed his eyes, and Jamie giggled silently.

When they reached Walnut Avenue, Violet stopped opposite the bungalow. "Oh," she said. "I didn't think. Mum's home."

Freddie had been thinking about it all day. Meeting Violet after school meant he wouldn't be able to sneak in when they got back.

She glanced down at Jamie. "Jay, say bye to Freddie." Jamie waved.

Violet leaned forward and hugged him. His upper body tensed. She was hugging him. Violet. "Wait by the courtyard wall," she whispered.

He nodded and waved them across the street. Then when they were safely inside, he did as she'd said and tiptoed down the side passage to wait behind the wall that enclosed her courtyard garden. If someone saw him, they'd be sure to think he was doing something sketchy. He prayed she wouldn't be long. She wasn't. Ten minutes later he heard her from the other side. "Can you make it over?"

Freddie looked up and down the alley. It was risky. Foolish. But, with great difficulty, he hauled himself up and tumbled down the other side. He landed on his elbow and had to stop himself from shouting. Violet hurried him inside and guarded the bedroom door while he clambered up into the attic. As he closed the hatch she waved up and mouthed, "Thanks."

An hour later, she tapped and lifted up a plate of lasagna. It just appeared, a hand, a plate, a wedge of homemade lasagna, and then she was gone. They were definitely becoming friends.

# 24

## FREDDIE

The day before Christmas Eve, Freddie went back to the Christmas fair, and approached the stall with the wooden trains. The man was there, and he smiled when Freddie approached him. "Ah, took up the challenge, did you?"

Freddie reached into his pocket and nervously produced the repurposed piece of wood that was now Violet's Christmas present. The man took a pair of glasses out of his apron pouch and placed them on the bridge of his nose. They made his eyes look bigger.

He held Freddie's carving for a long time, studying it. "What did you do this with?"

"Just a pocketknife, sir," Freddie replied, certain that was the wrong answer.

The man removed his glasses and folded his arms. "It's wonderful."

Freddie's mouth nearly dropped open. "Is it?"

The man nodded. "You're hired."

"I'm sorry, sir? I thought you said your friend...?"

The man laughed. "Firstly, stop calling me sir; my name's Frank. And secondly, I lied. Didn't want you hassling me if you weren't any good. But turns out, you are. So, if you get yourself a place at trade school and show me some references, you can start in September."

Freddie's legs felt wobbly, as if he needed to sit down before he fell down. "I don't know what to say."

The man looked at his watch and handed back Violet's present. "Just say thanks and contact me in the new year when you've sorted your school placement. I'm off for lunch." Then he looked behind him, called, "Lucy, watch the stall?" patted Freddie on the back, and strode off toward a German hot dog stand.

Freddie was numb. He couldn't believe what had just happened. For a while, he wandered aimlessly up and down the market stalls, trying to quell the bounce in his step and the grin on his face. But then he remembered that he still hadn't bought Jamie a gift.

He was heading in the direction of the bookshop— What had Violet said he liked? Pugs? There must've been a children's book with a pug in it—when he saw Gina, huddled on a bench near the traffic lights. A pang of guilt twisted his stomach. He hovered, hoping she'd get up and leave so he wouldn't have to decide whether to approach her or walk past. But Gina stayed put, bobbing her foot up and down on a crack in the pavement, and lit a cigarette. She pulled her scarf tighter around her throat and exhaled a slow plume of smoke. Freddie took a deep breath, shoved his hands into his pockets, and crossed to her side of the road.

Even when he was standing right in front of her, she didn't recognize him. She rested her elbow on her hip, cigarette pointing to the sky, and bit her cheek at him. "Can I help you with something?"

Freddie smiled and brushed his fingers through his hair.

Gina blinked. Then squinted.

"It's Freddie."

"Crap." Gina stood up and plucked the front of Freddie's suit, her lips spreading into a toothy grin. Then she tossed the cigarette to the floor and threw herself at him. She wrapped her arms around his neck and thumped his back. "Where've you been? It's been months."

"Long story," he said, shrugging.

Gina stood back and used the toe of her boot to stub out the cigarette. She glanced at her watch, "You comin' to The Kitchen?"

"I was just passing."

"Got somewhere to be?"

Freddie's hands were still in his pockets. "I... Sure, yeah, I'll come."

"Good."

\* \* \*

The Kitchen was run by St. Barnabas Church. On Tuesdays, Thursdays, and Sundays they used unwanted food from local supermarkets to host an open-door café where people could turn up, eat as much as they wanted, and pay whatever they were able to. They also had wash basins, toothbrushes, and toothpaste.

When Gina returned from out back, she was wearing an apron and holding a tray that carried two large bowls of stew. She deposited one at a table nearby, saying, "Enjoy, Melv. Don't wolf it down now, you hear?" then gave the second to Freddie. She slid onto the bench opposite him and gestured to the bowl. "Eat up."

Freddie wasn't hungry, but he ate anyway.

"So," said Gina, examining him, "you disappear for months and then turn up out the blue. You been in trouble?"

Freddie finished chewing, then said, "Just staying with friends."

"Fancy friends, by the look of you."

Freddie shuffled in his seat. "Not really."

"S'all right. I'm pleased for you," she said. And he knew she meant it. "I'm back home now, anyway. With Mum and that."

"That's great and is she...?"

"She's cut down. Not doing it in the evening no more. Just when me and the kids are out during the day. She sleeps it off in the afternoon. Even does tea most nights."

Freddie tried to feel happy for Gina, but he knew his smile fell short of being convincing.

"Here listen, bein' that you have fancy friends now—"

"They're not—"

"You know anything about those people, the ones who help animals? What're they called? RAC?"

Freddie tried to hide his smile. "I think you mean RSPCA?"

"Yeah. Them."

"What do you need them for?"

Gina sighed. "It's Aggie. Mum's bitch. She had pups a few months back. We should have had her done, but we never got 'round to it and next door's rotten Doberman mounted her. Poor girl. Anyway, we sold all the pups. Made sure they went to good homes. I interviewed people and everything...but this one little'n, he's been returned. Reckon the posh twat that took him didn't realize he'd have to train him not to shit on the carpet. Expected him to be perfect from day one. He's a real sweet dog. Just wants to be cuddled, really." Gina's voice had softened. "But Mum says we can't keep him, so I was wonderin' about those rescue people. Only thing is, we ain't got Aggie chipped so Mum's worried we'll get in trouble."

Freddie's mouth spoke before his brain had chance to catch up. "I'll take him."

Gina crossed her arms in front of her chest and narrowed her eyes. "Didn't know you even liked dogs."

"I don't. Well, I mean, I like dogs. I never had one. But the family who've been helping me, they've been after a puppy for a while. Their little boy's got...problems. They think it'll help him."

Gina's eyes widened. "He ain't violent?"

"No, no. He's only six. He finds social stuff a bit awkward. Gets really shy. That sort of thing."

Gina cocked her head. "Oh. Well, I suppose if you bring them over—"

"I can't. I mean, I'd like it to be a surprise. To thank them for their help." Freddie paused, then added, "You trust me, don't you, G?"

Gina thought for a moment, tapping her nails on the table. "All right. I'll bring him on Friday. Come back then, and he's yours."

"Friday's Christmas Eve."

Gina nodded. "We're doin' a turkey special."

"All right," he said. "I'll see you Friday."

\* \* \*

Walking back to the Johnsons', Freddie felt as though he was floating. He was picturing Jamie's face on Christmas morning, finding a puppy under the tree. And Violet's. And Ellie's. He hadn't quite figured out the logistics of getting the dog into the house and under the tree un-noticed, but he'd think of something, he was sure of it. And, in a way, he was helping Gina too, which helped to ease his guilt for not seeing or contacting her in so long.

Usually, when Violet deposited his dinner through the hatch, he just took it, silently, and returned the plate to the kitchen the next morning. That night, however, when Violet's hand appeared, Freddie took hold of it and peered down at her. Her eyes widened, and she glanced nervously toward the door—Ellie and Pete were still up.

"Sorry," he whispered. "I just... What are your plans over Christmas? I'm just trying to work out when I can, you know, come and go."

"Oh, I hadn't thought. Well, I finish school tomorrow; so does Jay. Mum's working till the twenty-third, and Dad...well, Dad will probably work the whole holiday."

A noise came from the hallway.

"I'll write the rest down," she said, already closing the hatch.

The next morning, on Violet's bed, was a postcard that read,

### Christmas Eve—Day

*Random aunties and uncles. Evening— Uncle Steve's. He's got a new girlfriend he's dying to show off. Usually leave at lunch- time and get back seven-ish.*

### Christmas Day—Morning
*Church with Grandad and Elsie (Dad's
stepmum) at nine. Dad hates it, but they
insist. Then eleven-ish we'll be back home
for presents and lunch and in all day.*

### Boxing Day
*Home all day.*

### Rest of Week
*Bit random until NYE.*

### NYE
*Usually party at Aisla's. Who knows this
year.*

*Your plans? Let me know so I can bring
food, etc.*

Freddie took a postcard from the stack he now kept
on his box table and scribbled,

### Christmas Eve
*Attic.*

### Christmas Day
*Attic.*

### Boxing Day
*Attic.*

### Rest of Week
*Attic.*

### NYE
*Attic OR Maldives. Still deciding.
Leftovers would be great.*

The Christmas Eve part was a lie. In fact, at four-thirty
he headed to meet Gina. He'd never been to Gina's house
but knew the estate where she lived. She met him in the
park by the swings.

"Mum'd ask for money if she saw you so I told her I was just gonna leave him outside the RSPCA place."

Freddie bent down to stroke the puppy. He was a big puppy. Black and shaggy, with chocolatey brown eyes and bushy tan eyebrows. "Hi, boy."

The puppy licked the back of Freddie's hand and sat down at his feet.

Gina raised an eyebrow. "Look at you—dog whisperer. He's never that quiet."

Freddie thanked her and made her take twenty pounds from him, even though he knew she'd probably give it straight to her mum.

"See you soon, yeah?"

"Promise."

"'Kay. Bye, Scruff."

"Is that his name?"

Gina shrugged. "Seems to answer to it."

* * *

As they walked back toward the Johnsons', Freddie told Scruff the plan. "Now, listen, boy. We're going to sleep outside tonight. It might be a bit chilly, so I've brought some blankets. Then, tomorrow morning, we'll sneak you in and put you under the tree. Okay?"

Scruff looked up at him and licked his lips.

"You hungry? We're heading for the park. We'll have something when we get there."

When they reached the bench Freddie had in mind, he took blankets, some dog treats, and a big pile of those hand warmers that only get hot when you take them out of the wrapper from his backpack. He made Scruff a bed next to him on the bench, stuffed it with the hand warmers, and pulled his coat a little closer.

Scruff didn't seem at all worried by the strangeness of it all. He just settled down, head on Freddie's knee, and slept. Freddie, however, didn't sleep. He'd forgotten how bitterly cold it was if you didn't keep moving. And he'd forgotten how luxurious his attic-room had felt when he'd first been ensconced in it. Even trapped in the darkness, waiting for a chance to escape after the Johnsons had returned home early, he'd been so incredibly grateful to be warm and dry.

At 4:00 a.m. it started to drizzle, so Freddie gathered their things and started walking again.

By six-thirty they were back at Walnut Avenue.

They paced up and down until eight when, finally, the Johnsons left, and Freddie was able to sneak them both in through the back door. In the living room, he clipped Scruff's leash to the radiator and attached an envelope to his collar. Then he said, "Merry Christmas, Scruff. Be good," and hurried himself back up into the attic.

# 25
## VIOLET

Church was dull, as always. Jamie yawned, and Violet spent most of the service wondering whether Elsie was wearing a wig or not and, if she was, whether it might be possible to blow really really hard and make it fall off.

Back home, they deposited their coats and shoes in the hallway and Jamie hurtled through to the living room. Then he stopped. He was staring at something.

"What is it, Jay?" Violet followed him. Then she stopped too.

Jamie grabbed her hand.

Their mum walked up behind them. "Guys, what are you—"

"You got us a dog!!!" Violet was yelling and she didn't care.

Jamie lurched forward and wrapped his arms around the big black puppy that was tied to the radiator. The puppy licked his face and wagged its tail, and then it and Jamie were in a fur-and-Jamie bundle on the floor and Jamie was crying silently with joy.

Violet joined them and ruffled the dog's ears, then she noticed the envelope tucked into its collar. Holding it, she looked up at their mum.

"Vi, I didn't... We didn't..." Their mum shouted toward the bathroom, where their dad was "washing the God" off his hands. "Pete?!"

For one glorious moment, Violet thought her father had surprised them all. But when their dad appeared, he looked so shocked that it could have been a tiger sitting in his living room instead of a puppy. Her parents didn't do this...

Violet opened the envelope. A postcard. She turned it over, but she already knew whose handwriting she would find:

*His name is Scruff. Please take care of him.*
*Love from Santa x*

# 26
## FREDDIE

Freddie lay with his ear pressed to the living room vent and a grin on his face for a very long time. He wished so badly that he could have seen Jamie's face, but he'd have to rely on Violet to tell him about it later.

For nearly an hour, the Johnsons had pondered loudly and excitedly, all except Pete, about who had brought this mystery dog into their house. Pete concluded it was Helen. Meddling. To which Ellie said, "Well we did speak about it briefly, but I still don't see how..."

At that point, Violet had interrupted. Freddie pictured her standing up and putting her hands purposefully on her hips. "Before we get attached—are we keeping him?"

Silence.

Pete started to say something, but then Ellie said, "Right. Okay. It's Christmas. And this wonderful, amazing gift has been given to us and, Pete, to be honest, I don't care that you're not excited about it."

Freddie imagined Violet raising an eyebrow at her mum's directness.

"Look how happy Jamie is and Violet and, well, and me as well. I say we thank Santa for this beautiful dog, and we keep him and love him. Because he needs a family. And, Pete, this family needs him."

After that speech, Pete didn't stand a chance. So, just like Freddie, Scruff stayed.

\* \* \*

It was nearly one in the morning when Violet tapped on the hatch and brought Freddie a plate of leftover Christmas dinner.

As she climbed up, she whispered, "I'm so sorry. I couldn't get away."

The Johnsons had enjoyed a picture-perfect Christmas Day. Church, dog, lunch, presents, board games, turkey sandwiches, more board games, a movie, and finally bed. And Freddie had enjoyed every second of it. At first, he thought it might make him feel worse. But it hadn't. He'd absorbed each distinguishable moment and let it play in his mind so that he almost felt as if he'd been there for it all.

Violet watched eagerly as Freddie started to eat his dinner. Earlier in the day, the smell of it had made him salivate, but now that it was cold and he was full from the chocolates and chips he'd bought himself, he didn't really feel like eating it. Especially the sprouts. But Violet seemed so pleased she'd smuggled it to him that he ate it anyway. Forcing it down with a smile.

When he finished, she took the plate, put it behind her, and gave him the most enormous hug. As she pulled away, he said, breathlessly, "What was that for?"

Violet laughed. "As if you don't know."

Freddie made a confused face.

"Scruff?"

"Who?" He was trying not to grin.

"Okay, fine. Play ignorant. But I know it was you. I don't know how you did it. But it was you, and it's amazing. So, thank you, Santa."

Freddie was blushing. A scene danced across his mind, a scene in which he brandished a sprig of mistletoe from behind his back and held it above Violet's head...but instead he reached under his pillow and took out the gift he'd bought her.

"I, um, this is for you. It's not much."

Violet was grinning, already unfolding the tissue paper. She did it slowly, as if she was savoring every moment, and Freddie wondered if this was how she'd opened all of her presents. Taking it out of its wrapping, she smiled and turned it over in her hands. "A wooden feather?"

Freddie leaned forward and turned it over for her. "It's a key chain, see, and it says..."

"*Hope*...like Emily Dickinson?"

Freddie nodded. She understood. He knew she would. "So, ah, so you always have a little piece of hope in your pocket."

"It's beautiful. Where did you find it?"

Freddie felt himself blush. "I, ah, I made it."

Violet was looking at him with an expression he hadn't seen before, and he couldn't quite decipher it. "You made this?"

"Mm."

"That's incredible. Thank you." There was a long pause while she looked at the little wooden feather, stroking the markings and the engraving on the back. Then she reached into the pocket of her cardigan. "This is yours. It's not wrapped though."

She handed him an iPod. Not an old classic kind—one that looked like an iPhone but wasn't. He immediately tried to hand it back. "Violet, no, I can't take this."

Violet tutted. "It's an old one, you doughnut. Mum gave it to me ages ago to sell. She said I could keep the cash, but I kept it in case my phone ever broke and I needed a music backup." She gestured to the iPod as if she was trying to convince him it was a good present. "I know you can't use it without Wi-Fi, but at least we could, you know, text and stuff when you're here."

Freddie was holding the iPod as if Violet had just given him a solid gold bullion.

"And here..." She took out a pair of headphones. "So you can listen to music and stuff."

Freddie turned away. Tears were clambering at the backs of his eyes, threatening to stream down his cheeks.

Violet cleared her throat awkwardly. "Sorry, it's a stupid—"

He turned back and wiped his eyes. "It's the nicest thing anyone has ever gotten me." He held it to his chest. How could something so ridiculous, an iPod for heaven's sake, suddenly make him feel human again? How could he ever make her see that she had just given him a piece of himself back? A lifeline. A window to the world outside the attic. He couldn't. So he just said, "Thank you," and hugged her back.

Violet laughed. "Wow. If that's your reaction to an extinct iPod with, like, barely any battery life, what on earth are you going to think of this...?" She was reaching behind her and handing him something else—this time, wrapped.

Freddie composed himself and placed the iPod gently on the sleeping bag next to him. Her second gift was a sweater. A gray, woolly, probably quite fashionable sweater.

"It wasn't expensive, but I figured all you have is your suit and your hoodie, and maybe something in between would be handy?"

Freddie smiled, relieved he hadn't started crying over a cheap gray sweater.

# 27
## FREDDIE & VIOLET

*VIOLET: How's it going?*
*FREDDIE: Oh, u know. Not bad. Busy busy.*
*VIOLET: We're out later. Will leave leftovers. Netflix*
*    password is EPVJ2013. Email: Family@TheJohnsons.*
*    com. U can use my profile.*
*FREDDIE: Family email? Cute.*
*VIOLET: Yeah. We're losers.*
*FREDDIE: Happy Boxing Day. Loser.*
*VIOLET: Says the boy in the ceiling . . .*
*FREDDIE: Ouch.*
*VIOLET: ;-)*

# 28
## VIOLET

Usually, Violet spent New Year's Eve with Aisla. Her parents always had an extravagant party. Her mum, dad, and Jamie would be invited. They'd all sleep over and have breakfast in Aisla's glossy kitchen, then swim in the indoor pool, go for a walk if it was sunny...every year for four years it had been the same. But this year, when her mum called on the twenty-seventh to ask what was happening, Aisla's mum told her that they were keeping things "low key" this year.

Violet knew her mum didn't believe it either because she hugged her tighter than normal as she said, "I always found those parties over the top. New Year's Eve is better when it's small, chilled out. We'll stay home, the four of us, and we'll eat junk food and watch movies in our onesies."

Violet sniffed. She was trying not to cry. "Dad doesn't have a onesie."

"Well then, we'd better buy him one." Her mum took out her phone, and in less than two minutes had ordered a Grumpy (from *Snow White*) onesie that made Violet laugh so much she thought her bladder might burst.

\* \* \*

On New Year's Eve, her mum set up everything. The blow-up mattress was in front of the TV with duvets and pillows. There was popcorn, a stack of old DVDs, mini pizza bites, sausage rolls, pineapple and cheese on sticks—Jamie's request—and a tub of chocolates left over from Christmas. Jamie was bouncing up and down on the mattress with Scruff, when their dad entered the room wearing his onesie. The utter humiliation on his face simply made it funnier, and Jamie and their mum clapped with joy. Violet took a photo and sent it to Aunt Helen.

It was seven-thirty, and they were still trying to decide what to watch when their dad's phone rang. His ringtone sliced through the happy atmosphere like a knife, and their mum whispered, "Not work, Pete, please..."

Their d shook his head and was about to silence the call when he said, "It's not work. It's my dad."

He stumbled up from the air mattress and took his phone into the hallway.

"Why's Grandad calling?" Violet asked her mum. Their grandad *never* called, and they'd only seen him that morning.

"I don't know, love; maybe we left something at their place earlier?" Their mum didn't sound convinced.

After less than a minute, their dad came back into the room, unbuttoning the onesie with one hand and waving his phone in the other. "It's Elsie, she's...well, they don't know, maybe a stroke? Dad could barely get his words out. I've never heard him like that, El—"

"All right, all right, love." Their mum was standing up and guiding their dad into the hall. "Which hospital are they at? We'll meet them. Let's just get changed..."

Jamie was twirling his fingers in Scruff's fur, and Scruff was gently licking him. Violet put her arm around her little brother and hugged him to her. Neither of them liked Elsie very much. She and their grandad had moved in together before Jamie had even been born, but perhaps their grandma's dislike of her had rubbed off on them and they'd never warmed to her. Even when she'd tried to soften them up with too many cookies.

Her dad liked her though. He'd always said she was good for his father. A bit younger, a bit more energetic. Still in her eighties, but the kind of eighty-year-old who did evening classes and went to Zumba. The total opposite of how their grandma had been.

Surely, they couldn't lose another grandparent. Not yet.

When their mum came back, she was wearing her coat and clutching an overnight bag. "Violet, I'm so sorry. Can you look after Jamie? I don't know how long we'll be. We'll probably have to take Grandad home and stay with him."

"He can't be on his own," their dad said, grabbing the car keys from their hook.

"I know," their mum turned to him. "That's what I was saying to Violet. That we'll stay with him."

"He can't come here. He'd have to stay in Mum's old room, and he wouldn't want that."

Their mum put her hand on their dad's forearm and made him look at her. "Pete. It's okay." She smiled. "It's going to be okay." Then she took the car keys. "I'll drive. Violet, we'll call you, all right?"

Violet nodded. "'Course. Go. Tell Elsie..."

Their mum nodded and steered their dad out of the front door. "Lock the door, Vi."

# 29
## FREDDIE & VIOLET

*VIOLET: Change of plan. Just me and J tonight. Wanna join us? Loads of food.*
*FREDDIE: You sure?*
*VIOLET: 110%*

# 30
## FREDDIE

Freddie looked at himself in the small, round mirror that was balanced next to his plastic wash basin. He was wearing the sweater Violet had given him for Christmas. It suited him, but he'd been wearing it for three days now because it reminded him of her, and he was worried it was smelling a bit stale. He also had more stubble than normal. He hadn't been expecting to see her. He thought he'd be spending New Year's Eve alone with his books.

When he entered the living room, Jamie hurtled toward him and wrapped his arms around Freddie's legs. Scruff wasn't far behind, jumping up and down and making a high-pitched sound that belonged more to a mouse than a chunky black puppy.

Violet smiled at him and held her arms out to her sides, laughing at herself. She was wearing a purple unicorn, all-in-one pajama thing that looked so ridiculous it was cute. "I wanted to change, but Jamie wouldn't let me."

"I'm glad you didn't," he said, resisting the urge to kiss her on the cheek. "I like it."

As they sat down on the blow-up mattress and started narrowing down their film selection, Violet told him what had happened. "I'm sorry," he said, glancing at Jamie.

Jamie had stopped speaking when their gran had died. Surely, whatever was happening with their step-gran wasn't good.

Violet mouthed, "He's okay." Then, to her little brother, she said, "Okay, dude. You choose."

Jamie chose *The Lego Batman Movie*, and Violet rolled her eyes. "Seriously?"

He nodded enthusiastically, waggling the DVD case at her.

"I haven't seen it," Freddie said, taking the case from Jamie and putting the disc in the DVD player. "Is it any good?"

Jamie nodded again and patted the space next to him for Freddie to get closer. Violet brought the popcorn and the mini pizzas down from the coffee table and squeezed in on the other side of Jamie but, almost immediately, Scruff assumed that as the food had been brought down to his level it was now fair game and ran off with two mini pizzas dangling from his mouth.

Violet chased after him, but he wedged himself be-hind the armchair in the corner of the room, growling in a comical and utterly un-menacing way until she gave up and let him just eat the damn things. It took her and Freddie a further ten minutes to coax him out, by which time Jamie was in fits of giggles and the popcorn had spilled all over the duvet.

Freddie volunteered to take Scruff outside for a bathroom break while Violet scooped up the popcorn and located a plastic dog toy cone that she filled with cream cheese and dog treats.

"Right," she said, flopping down next to Jamie. "That should keep Scruff busy for at least two minutes, so let's get on with this blessed movie."

Jamie grinned mischievously and snuggled down as Freddie pressed play on the remote. Holding it, he remembered the day he'd looked at rooms on their TV. Back then, he'd known them only as the kids in the photo frame. Never, in his wildest imaginings, would he have thought he'd end up like this.

* * *

The film ended just before midnight. Jamie had fallen asleep less than twenty minutes in, but neither of them had wanted to move him. Now, he was stretched out, mouth open, head resting on Violet's tummy and legs curled next to Freddie's chest. Scruff was on Freddie's feet and was snoring loudly. Violet's phone pinged.

"It's Mum. Elsie's okay. Not a stroke, but they're keeping her overnight. Mum and Dad are staying at Grandad's, but they'll be back tomorrow morning."

Freddie could see the relief in her face. "I'm glad she's okay."

"Me too."

Last year, Freddie had spent New Year's Eve in the park with a bottle of vodka. He hadn't opened it. In the end, he'd given it to a bunch of twenty-somethings in 80's costumes. But he'd wanted to. There had been a thick mizzle in the air that had made his clothes smell strange and his bones ache and, just before midnight, he had walked to the multi-story parking ramp at the end of the main street and climbed up through the urine-coated stairwells until he'd reached the top floor. Fireworks had been let off all over town. The skyline had fizzled with them. The clock tower had begun its count down.

Taking off his jacket and backpack, Freddie had draped them over the hood of a black BMW and climbed up onto the bare concrete wall. He had dangled his legs over the edge and stretched his arms out sideways. He had breathed deep into his lungs, pictured his mum and Amy.

And then he had noticed the safety netting below him. He had almost laughed.

* * *

Violet turned the TV to the channel showing the fireworks in London. Freddie watched her count under her breath: five...four...three...two...one...

"Happy New Year, Freddie," she whispered.

"Happy New Year, Violet."

# JANUARY

# 31
## VIOLET

The first day back at school after Christmas was a Friday. She liked it when that happened. She hadn't spoken to Jeanette since the incident in hallway. She'd texted over the break. Jeanette had read it, the blue ticks had said so, but she hadn't replied so Violet was surprised when she walked up to her at the gates.

"Hi." She was wearing a Christmas sweater. In January.

"Hi," Violet replied.

"Sorry I went AWOL. It wasn't you. It was family stuff." Violet nodded.

"Mr. Smythe wants to see us."

Violet inhaled sharply through her nose. "Why?"

"Oh, I dunno." Jeanette was attempting sarcasm. "Maybe something to do with having buckets of mulch thrown all over us?"

"Oh."

Jeanette motioned toward the school.

"He wants to see us now?"

"Yep."

* * *

Mr. Smythe spent the whole of first period telling both Violet and Jeanette that they might as well explain what was going on because he had looked at the CCTV footage and Christopher Parker was not going to be getting away with his abhorrent behavior. Jeanette said very little, except that she'd never had a problem with Chris before and that, for some reason, he seemed to hate Violet.

Violet said she didn't know what she'd done to upset him and that she really didn't want to take things any further as it would just make everything worse. She just wanted to forget about it.

But Mr. Smythe was having none of it. "I'm sorry, girls. I simply can't allow this kind of behavior to continue. I'm going to call Chris's parents and yours, and we'll get to the bottom of this."

Both Violet and Jeanette protested but the principal was adamant, and the following Wednesday after school, Violet found herself waiting outside Mr. Smythe's office on a line of navy-blue chairs with Chris and his parents. For some reason Millie and Kyra, his sidekicks, had been excused and Jeanette wasn't there yet either.

Her mum was tapping her foot nervously on the floor, still annoyed that her dad hadn't canceled his meeting to accompany them. "Violet, I wish you would just tell me what this is about."

"It's nothing, Mum. They're making a big deal of nothing."

When they entered Mr. Smythe's office, Jeanette was already there, but she was alone—no parents. Mr. Smythe was doing his best "this is very serious" face and had already lined up five chairs in front of his desk. As they sat down, he turned his computer screen so it was facing them. "Before I say anything," he said, "I want you all to watch this."

Violet could feel her insides shrinking. She knew what they were about to watch, and she didn't want to look but felt like she had to. There, in full color, from a bird's-eye view, was the film of her and Jeanette rounding the corner into the math hallway. The camera was pointing in their direction and caught the expression on their faces perfectly—shock, fear, and a slow awareness of what was about to happen to them.

When Chris and the two girls threw their buckets of mulch, her mum let out an audible gasp. Jeanette hunched her shoulders and folded her arms across her middle. Violet looked over at Chris's parents, expecting them to be horrified, but they were both sitting with very straight faces and their hands clasped in their laps. When Mr. Smythe pressed Stop Chris's mum looked up at him and said, "Can you tell me why the two girls in this video aren't here?"

Mr. Smythe put one hand in his pocket and turned the monitor back toward him with the other. "Because, Mrs. Parker, the girls are being dealt with separately."

Mrs. Parker narrowed her eyes, and Mr. Parker looked at his son with an expression that bordered on disgust.

Chris hung his head, shrugged, and said something

unintelligible.

"Listen, if Christopher was involved in this, then there must be a very good reason. These two girls must've antagonized him." Mrs. Parker was sitting very upright in her chair, not looking at Violet or Jeanette or Violet's mum but waving her hand at them.

Violet could feel that her mum was about interrupt.

"I'm sorry, but whatever Violet did, I hardly think it would justify having buckets of God-knows-what thrown all over her?!"

Mr. Smythe sat down in his big comfortable looking chair on wheels and exhaled slowly. "Mrs. Johnson, I've spoken to Violet and Jeanette, but they're understandably reluctant to tell me the whole story. So, we're at a bit of an impasse, so to speak."

He looked over at Mr. and Mrs. Parker, then concentrated his gaze on Chris. "I am aware, though, that there has been *animosity* toward Violet for quite a while."

Chris wasn't looking him in the eye so Mr. Smythe leaned forward on his desk and, intertwining his fingers, said, "Christopher—Chris—why don't you give us your side of the story so we can get to the bottom of this and stop it from getting any worse. I'm aware of some hurtful content going around on social media too, and I'd hate for the police to get involved."

Violet shrank into her chair, wishing she could meld into it and disappear. Every day since the bucket incident, she'd been tagged in posts that she told herself she wouldn't look at, then did. They were stupid, childish—things like a seal with lipstick, an orangutan with a purple wig, someone on TV having green slime thrown over them. On their own, they wouldn't have bothered her, but day after day after day it was becoming a bit much. She'd deleted all the apps from her phone over Christmas and hadn't yet reinstalled them, but if Mr. Smythe knew what was happening then it must've still been going on. Her mum took hold of her hand and squeezed it.

Chris folded his arms, looked sideways at Violet, then tried to make himself look bigger in his chair. "Basically, she's a tease. She invited me over, made it clear that something was going to happen, and then when we started to do stuff she backed out."

Violet closed her eyes and felt sick. Then she realized what was coming. How did she not think of this before?

Chris was looking at his parents, doing big eyes and a woeful expression. "And then some guy appeared out of nowhere and basically beat me up and threw me out on the street."

Mrs. Parker's mouth had fallen open as if the shocking part of the story was that someone had manhandled her precious little boy. Her mum was still clasping Violet's hand and clasped even tighter when Mrs. Parker rounded on her and said, "Was this your husband? Did he assault my son?"

Her mum's cheeks were growing redder by the second. "It seems to me that if anyone *assaulted* someone it was your pig of a son!"

Mrs. Parker nearly jumped up out of her chair, but Mr. Parker put his hand on her forearm and told her to sit down.

Violet's mum softened her voice and turned to Violet. "Violet. You need to tell us what happened."

Violet looked over at Jeanette, and finally Jeanette

met her eyes and nodded. "Just tell them, Vi. It's not your fault."

Violet sighed and angled herself in her chair so she was only looking at her mum. "It was the night you and Dad went away. I texted Chris and invited him over. I didn't invite him over for—that—not like he said. Chris was nice to me on my first day. We spoke on the bus and then at the fireworks, and I just thought we would hang out. I didn't know anyone else, so..." she trailed off.

"Okay. And what about this 'guy'? Where did he come from? Because it certainly wasn't your father; he was with me."

Violet sucked in her breath and prepared herself. "His name's Freddie. He's...my boyfriend." The words came out stuttering and jittery and as if they weren't really true, but her mum didn't seem to notice.

"Boyfriend?"

Chris was shaking his head as it was all a load of garbage, but Violet kept talking. "I invited him over to meet Chris. I thought they'd get along. He was outside, and he heard what was happening. Heard me shout. So, he came in and he rescued me, and if he hadn't been there..." This part was true, and her skin tightened with the memory of it, like she was wearing a cold, clammy wetsuit.

Her mum sat back in her chair and told her they would deal with the secret boyfriend, and the inviting people over when her and her dad were out, later. But, for now, she wanted to know what Mr. Smythe was going to do about the situation.

Chris's mum was outraged, said Violet had set Chris up, that it was all a joke. Chris's dad said nothing, just silently seethed and, after they were told Chris would be suspended for a week, put his head in his hands and sighed.

* * *

Climbing into her mum's car and shutting the doors, Violet waited for the impending explosion. But her mum turned to her and, stroking the side of her face, said, "Vi. You should have talked to me. You know you can talk to me."

Violet pulled back and shook her head. "I'm sorry. For inviting him over."

"That was silly, but I think you learned your lesson."

"I am sorry." Her voice wavered.

"I know." Her mum turned the keys in the ignition and started pulling into the road. "Now, listen. Boyfriend? Where did he come from?"

# 32
## FREDDIE & VIOLET

VIOLET: U awake?
FREDDIE: Nope.
VIOLET: Need a favor.
FREDDIE: ???
VIOLET: Mum knows what happened with Chris.
FREDDIE: Shit.
VIOLET: Had meeting with the principal about bullying.
   Chris tried to make it sound like u beat him up.
FREDDIE: *bulging arm emoji*
VIOLET: Need u to be my boyfriend—Fake Boyfriend—
   Fake Boyfriend who comes to dinner and meets my
   nosey parents.
FREDDIE: Like, come to the front door? Pretend I'm
   not living in ur attic? Eat at the table? That kind of
   dinner?
VIOLET: Yep. Will u?

FREDDIE: *Can't you just say we broke up?*

VIOLET: *Should have. Didn't think . . . And I've kind of already said you will . . . Tomorrow.*

FREDDIE: *How do u know I don't have plans for tomorrow?*

VIOLET: *'Cause u live in my attic. Ur plans are sit in dark, speak to mice, eat crappy cereal bar, repeat.*

FREDDIE: *Thought u needed my help?*

VIOLET: *Pleaaaasssssseeeee.*

FREDDIE: *One more time?*

VIOLET: *Pleeeeaaaaaseeee.*

FREDDIE: *OK.*

# 33
## VIOLET

Violet's legs were wobbling as she went to the door to let Freddie in. She'd thought he might be wearing his suit, but he must have changed in town because he was in jeans, the gray sweater she'd bought him for Christmas, and a gray coat she didn't recognize.

"Hi," she said, leaning forward to kiss him on the cheek because that's what she would have done if he really was her boyfriend.

He looked nervous and stood stock-still when she kissed him. When she pulled away, he was blushing, but before she could tease him for it her mum came into the hallway, all smiles, wearing an apron—when did she *ever* wear an apron?

"Well," she said in a weirdly upbeat voice, "this must be Freddie?"

Freddie extended his hand, and her mum shook it.

"It's, ah, really good to meet you, Mrs. Johnson. Thanks for inviting me."

Her mum laughed. "Well, now that Violet's not keeping you a secret anymore, I hope to be inviting you around more often."

Violet rolled her eyes, and as they walked through to the kitchen, she mouthed, "Sorry," in Freddie's direction. He shook his head at her as if it didn't matter, and when they plonked themselves awkwardly on the sofa while her mum finished dinner, he turned to her and said, "Your mum's great. Don't apologize."

"She's just..."

"Looking out for you."

"Mm."

Dinner was risotto. Posh risotto with shavings of parmesan and crispy bacon bits and something orange that might have been butternut squash on top. Her mum had been cooking it for at least two hours, but despite her emphasizing to her dad that Freddie was coming over and it was important he was here, he wasn't.

"Well," said her mum, trying not to sound exhausted. "We better get started—it's not the kind of thing that will keep. It dries out. Vi, can you call your brother?"

Violet stood still and yelled, "JAMIE!"

"Not quite what I meant."

"You said *call*..."

Seconds later, Jamie wandered into the room and, seeing Freddie, hurtled himself forward and gave him an enormous leg hug.

Her mum frowned. "Oh, have you two...? Have you met?"

Violet bit her lip and, before Freddie could answer,

said curtly, "Yes. Freddie went with me and Jamie to Gran's grave. We took flowers."

"Oh, you didn't say you went to the grave."

Violet shrugged. "Didn't seem important."

She was aware she was being spiky toward her mother, but she couldn't help it. The whole situation was putting her on edge, and she wasn't sure whether it was because she didn't want her mum to find out about Freddie living in their attic or because she wanted her to like him. And if she did want her mum to like him, why? Why should it matter? He was just Freddie. He'd be gone soon.

"Violet?" Her mum was speaking to her.

"Huh?"

"I said sit down?"

She did as she was told and helped herself to a big scoop of risotto from the pan in the center of the table, indicating that Freddie should do the same. He was very reserved with his portion, a little too reserved for someone who was the hungriest of all of them.

They were only a few spoonfuls in when the inevitable questioning began. Violet had expected it, and Freddie clearly had too because he'd been avoiding eye contact with her mother and concentrating mainly on his food.

"So, Freddie, Violet hasn't told me much about you. Are you studying?"

Freddie set down his fork and looked Ellie straight in the eyes. They had rehearsed this. Violet had told him he needed to sound confident. "Not yet. I wasn't sure what I wanted to do so I'm just working at the moment. Hoping to start at the college in September, if I can decide which course."

Her mum smiled, but it was the kind of smile that implied she wasn't overly impressed by the fact Freddie had so little direction. "Violet's hoping to do art there, aren't you, Vi?"

Violet narrowed her eyes. "Freddie knows this, Mum."

"And what about your parents, Freddie? What do they do?"

This was the one. The worst one. Freddie's face quivered.

"Mum, why does that matter?"

Her mum was about to answer, but Freddie interjected. "It's okay, Vi. Your mum just wants to know who you're hanging out with."

She saw him inhaling deeply and purposefully. He scraped his fork around his plate. "My mum died when I was ten. So, it's just my dad, and I don't really get along with my step-mum. They moved away a while ago."

Her mum's face dropped, and Violet felt like shouting, "Hah! Now you feel bad for prying, right?!" But then she realized Freddie was telling the truth. She'd never asked him about his life *before*. She'd always figured he would tell her if and when he was ready to. And this sudden, stark, tragic fact made the risotto she was eating feel thick and gloopy in her mouth. She forced herself to swallow and took a swig of water.

"I'm so sorry," her mum said, meaning it.

"It's okay," Freddie replied, looking at Violet.

No, it's not, she thought.

Violet was trying to think of something to say that wasn't "How did she die?" when Scruff came bounding into the room. He made a beeline for Freddie and practically jumped into his lap.

Her mum smiled. "Well, Freddie, you certainly are popular."

Freddie was rubbing Scruff's ears. "Just good with dogs, I guess," he said, visibly relaxing.

Her mum started to clear the plates, and Freddie offered to help but Jamie tugged at his sleeve. "Yes, bud?"

Jamie waved his arms to get Scruff's attention and then patted both hands on his thighs to motion "come here". Scruff obeyed immediately, and Jamie brandished one of the everlasting supply of dog treats that was constantly squirreled away in his pocket, waving it in the air.

"Sit."

Violet gasped. Her mum froze.

Again, a small delicate voice, a voice they'd almost forgotten the sound of, said, "Sit."

"Jamie?" Their mum turned around. Violet was gripping Freddie's arm so hard she knew her fingernails would leave imprints.

Gently, Freddie removed Violet's hand and scooched his chair closer to Jamie's. "That's awesome, Jamie. You taught him that?"

Jamie nodded, grinning. He had risotto on his chin and a missing front tooth, and Violet felt so proud of him she thought her heart was going to leap right out of her chest.

"Can you show me again?" Freddie asked, glancing at Violet.

Jamie took out another treat.

"Sit."

God what a perfect word. What a perfect, wonderful word.

A few minutes later, Freddie and Jamie were in the

living room and Freddie was showing Jamie how to make Scruff shake hands. Jamie hadn't said anything else, but when Violet offered to help their mum dry the dishes she looked up and realized her mother was crying.

"Mum?"

Her mum turned to her, smiling through the tears. "Vi...I just..."

Violet hugged her. It wasn't the sort of thing they normally did, but in that moment, it was the only thing that said what they were both feeling.

Sniffing and wiping her nose on her apron, her mum pulled away. "Honestly, Vi, when I find the fairy godmother who left that dog under our tree...I'm going to...I don't know...bake her the biggest cake in the world." She laughed, turning to look at Jamie and Scruff and Freddie. "He *spoke*, Violet. Because of that smelly fur ball. He actually spoke."

Violet wanted so badly to say, "It was Freddie! Freddie is the fairy godmother. Isn't he wonderful? Look at what he's done for us!" But instead, she whispered, "Shall we call his therapist?"

Her mum shook her head. "No. Definitely not. We'll just let him do it in his own time. Right?"

"What about Dad? Do we tell Dad?"

Her mum paused and wrung the damp dishcloth between her fingers. "Yes. Of course. Of course, we do."

* * *

They said good night to Freddie at eight-thirty. Her dad still wasn't home, but Jamie's triumph meant her mum barely seemed to have noticed. Showing Freddie

out of the front door and hugging him goodbye felt so
normal, so unextraordinary that Violet had to remind
herself he would, in a minute, be sneaking back in over
her courtyard wall.

When the door was closed, she went into the living room and told her mum she was going to bed. Her
mum looked up from the sofa, where she was cuddling
a sleeping Jamie and smiled. "Night, love."

"Night."

"And, Vi?"

"Mm?"

"Freddie is lovely."

Yes, she thought, he is.

# 34
## FREDDIE

After leaving through the front door for the first time, Freddie crossed the street, walked to the bus stop, then looped back and waited behind Violet's courtyard wall. About half an hour later, a twisted and knotted-together bedsheet appeared over the wall, indicating it was okay to come back over.

Freddie tugged on the sheet. It held firm so he used it to lever himself over the wall. Again, he fell on his elbow. He needed to get better at that.

Violet rolled up the sheet and ushered him inside, shoving it under her bed. When she stood up, she was looking at him differently. He scuffed his left foot against his right, then glanced up at the ceiling. "Well, I better..."

Violet twitched her nose and repositioned her glasses. He wished she would always wear them. "Can I come up for a bit?"

Freddie frowned before he could stop himself.

"Sorry. You've had enough of me for one evening."

"No, no it's not that. What about your mum?"

Violet folded her arms, tucking her hands under her armpits. "Dad just got back. They're arguing."

"Then be my guest," he said, waving toward the bookcase. "Ladies first."

Before climbing up, Violet wedged her desk chair under her door to buy time in case Ellie or Pete came looking for her. Although she told him she was ninety-nine percent certain they wouldn't.

Leaving the hatch hanging open, Freddie jumped up after her and offered her the comfiest area of the sleeping bag nest. "Why are they arguing? Because he missed dinner?"

"Yeah. He missed you. And Jamie's word."

Freddie smiled, remembering it. "That was incredible."

"Yeah, it was. And it was because of you."

"Me?"

"You got Scruff for him. You knew it was what he needed. How did you know?"

"I heard your mum one time, talking to 'H'?"

"That's my Auntie Helen."

"Well, Helen said she'd seen a TV show about it, but your mum said your dad would never allow it. Then just before Christmas, my friend Gina asked me if I knew anyone who could help with this puppy she needed to rehouse, and it kind of just fell into place, I guess." He couldn't be sure, but it felt as if Violet was edging a little closer to him.

"Well, thank you. And thank you for coming to dinner."

"I enjoyed it."

Violet scoffed and tutted. "I'm almost certain that's a lie."

"No. Really. It was great."

"Mum likes you."

"Does she?"

"Yeah. So maybe this is all a good thing. Now, you can actually come in through the front door sometimes. And if any neighbors see you sneaking back in after, it's fine because, even if they do tell Mum, the worst that will happen is she'll be mad that I'm letting my boyfriend in after hours."

"Fake boyfriend."

"Exactly."

Freddie yawned. He didn't mean to, but it slipped out, and the second it did he could have kicked himself because Violet looked at her phone and said she would leave him in peace.

This time, she didn't hug him as she left because they were half-crouching right next to the hatch and it would have been awkward. But almost as soon as the hatch closed, his iPod lit up. *Meant to say … …* The three dots that told him she was typing, and retyping appeared, disappeared, appeared again. *If u want to talk about ur mum, I'm here.*

He did. He really did want to talk about her. He was bursting to. But if he talked about her, he'd talk about his father and Janet and Amy, and then Violet would know what he'd done. And that would be the end. His thumbs hovered over the keyboard.

FREDDIE: Thank u.

VIOLET: No rush.

FREDDIE: Night, Vi.

**VIOLET: Night, FTFB.**
**FREDDIE: ??**
**VIOLET: Freddie The Fake Boyfriend.**
**FREDDIE: Maybe one day it'll be FTRB.**

Shit. He'd pressed send before he'd even thought about it. She must've known what he meant. Freddie The Real Boyfriend. As if he'd said it? Written it down? This was basically him declaring that he liked her. That he, the boy living in her attic, liked her.

**VIOLET: Maybe**

# 35
## VIOLET

In the first few weeks after Freddie had become her fake boyfriend, not much changed. Violet "invited" him over for dinner a couple of times, but that was the limit of his interaction with her family. On the other nights, she continued to sneak him leftovers and he had started leaving books on the bed for her now too—always ones from the second-hand book shop, always with a note explaining when he'd first read it and why he thought she'd like it. They texted sometimes too. But their conversations were brief and never about anything serious.

He hadn't mentioned his plan for leaving, and Violet hadn't pushed him about it yet because, in truth, she didn't mind him being there. It had started to feel kind of...nice. He was her secret. Everything else in her life felt brash and exposed because, despite his best efforts, Mr. Smythe's interventions had done little to stop

Chris from taunting her. Each time a vicious social media account was taken down, a new one sprung up. She was trying her best to ignore it, but it was becoming harder each day.

Jeanette helped. She waltzed around the school as if it really didn't bother her in the slightest that she was made fun of. Violet suspected it was all a bit of an act because no one could really be that oblivious, but she was trying to let Jeanette's attitude rub off on her. The way she wore whatever clothes she liked, not caring a bit whether they were fashionable. The way she spoke loudly about her musical theatre ambitions and performed renditions of songs no one had ever heard of, frequently and publicly. Violet knew she should try to be more like that. She knew she shouldn't care what Chris and his minions thought of her. But she did. And Freddie was a distraction from it all because, instead of thinking about what was going on at school, she thought about him.

She spent her days imagining what he was doing. She didn't like to picture him in his suit because it didn't feel like the real him. She liked it when he was Freddie who came to dinner—in jeans and, usually, the gray sweater she'd bought him. And when he was Freddie who sent the kind of texts that made her snort her soft drink out through her nose because they were so funny. She also liked it when he was Freddie with the sad eyes and the secret past, and she was becoming more and more desperate to know about it. She'd promised she wouldn't ask. But maybe the things she wasn't asking were standing in the way of them becoming more...whatever it was she wanted them to become.

So, that evening, when her mum asked her when she was next going to invite Freddie for dinner, Violet told her he'd be coming over on Saturday and that he'd probably be there most of the day. Their mum smiled and said, "That's nice, love," and Jamie, who had been speaking a new word every day or so, said, "Freddie's my friend."

"Is he?" Violet laughed.

Jamie nodded and shoveled a forkful of spaghetti into his mouth. "Second."

"He's your second-best friend?"

Jamie nodded again.

Violet smiled, "Aw. That's nice, Jay, and who's your first?"

Foolishly, she expected him to say it was her, but he waved his fork toward the dog basket by the radiator and said, "Scruff! Silly!"

# 36
## FREDDIE

After his first Saturday with the Johnsons, Freddie returned to the attic with a head full of noise, a full belly, and the feeling that he was dreaming and would, at any moment, wake up. It had been so long since he'd been around that kind of family life. The business of it: Jamie careening in and out with books, his scooter, a miniature football, and one hundred and one other reasons for Freddie to stop talking to Violet and pay attention to him instead; Ellie tidying up around them, putting laundry in the washing machine, making lunch, then flopping down on the sofa and shooing them away so she could have a cup of tea in peace.

Pete hadn't been there, but at least his absence hadn't filled the house with a sense of dread at what kind of state he'd be in when he returned. He'd be late and tired, but he wouldn't be so drunk he passed out on the living room floor. Freddie shivered as he remembered how his Saturdays at home used to be. The kind of weekend the Johnsons had was a distant fuzzy memory, one that he'd long stopped wishing for, and he rarely allowed himself to think about them.

But now, because of Violet, he'd had one. A perfectly average day. Boring to some. He and Violet had simply sat in her room and talked for most of it. She'd shown him a sketch she was working on and a biography about Emily Dickinson. "Apparently she had a penchant for wearing white. Maybe I should do that."

"Or purple to match your hair," he'd said, trying to be humorous.

Violet had rolled her eyes at that. "Too cliched. But I've decided, if I'm going to be an artist, I need to start being okay with being different."

"Isn't everyone different?" he'd said, not really understanding what she meant.

"Yeah, but everyone at school is different in the same way. I need to stand out. I need to find my *thing*."

"Your thing?"

"Yes. Like, this girl Jeanette. I guess she's a friend. She's obsessed with musical theatre. She's determined to be in the West End, and she doesn't care if she looks like a lunatic whirling around hallways singing *Evita* or whatever."

"So, you're going to, what? Tuck a paintbrush behind your ear, wear a splattered apron, and yell, 'I'm an artist!'?"

"Obviously not. That's ridiculous." She'd sighed and looked a little less upbeat. "I just mean that I need to stop caring what people think of me, be true to myself, that's all."

Freddie genuinely couldn't imagine anyone thinking Violet was anything other than wonderful. He usually refrained from asking her questions that were too personal in case she started asking him things back, but something in the way she'd dropped her shoulders and was rubbing her thumb nervously across her palm had made him break his own rule. "Is Chris still giving you a hard time?"

Violet had shrugged and twitched her nose. "Not really. It's nothing."

And that had made Freddie mad. Really mad. He had wanted to storm out, then and there, track Chris down, and what? What could he do? He'd managed to stand up to Chris in Violet's living room, but he was pretty sure he'd lose if it came down to a fistfight between them.

He was still weighing up his options, listening to the rain and, not for the first time, thanking whoever it was he thanked silently in his head that he wasn't outside, when Violet tapped on the hatch. He opened it and helped her up. She looked at the inside of the roof. "Wow, you can really hear it up here, huh?"

Freddie nodded and shifted over so there was space for her at the end of the sleeping bag. She sat down, crossed her legs, and said, "Could we turn the lights off? And just...listen for a while?"

Freddie usually left the fairy lights on as long as possible, but for Violet he said, "Okay," and flicked them off.

With the bungalow below them in utter darkness, there was not a grain of light in the attic. Freddie couldn't see Violet, but he could feel her. The warmth of her, her energy. They sat in silence for a long time, listening to the rain pummeling the roof and the walls. Then, Violet said, "Just so you know. It's not because I'm not interested or because I don't care."

Freddie wished he could see her. "What do you mean?"

"The reason I don't ask about your life before you came here. It's not because I don't care. It's because I do—I don't want you to feel like you have to tell me. Not unless you want to."

He didn't know what to say. She didn't know. She couldn't know. If she did, she'd never want to be this close to him ever again.

Violet didn't say anything else, she just dropped back down onto her bed, closed the hatch, and left him with her words, hanging like lanterns in the gloom of his hiding space.

* * *

The next morning, instead of putting on his suit and going into town, Freddie put on his jeans and his gray sweater and headed to the library. On one of the public computers, he created a new Facebook account using the email address Violet had set up for him on his iPod. He wasn't interested in opening up his real—dormant— account. It would be like seeing a version of what his life might have been if he hadn't destroyed it.

On his new, empty timeline, he searched for Violet's school football team. She'd mentioned that Chris was a part of it, and it didn't take long to track him down by looking through photographs of their last practice. Chris's profile was on tight lockdown, but some of his pictures included a middle-aged couple who were very clearly his parents. Half an hour's googling later, Freddie plugged Chris Parker's home address into his iPod and went to find Gina.

When he arrived at The Kitchen, she was washing up. She had her back to him and, when she turned, she had a large, greenish bruise on her left cheek. She cocked her head at him, defiantly, daring him to comment on it. But he knew better. Instead, he said, "G, you know that neighbor of yours with the Doberman? Do you think he'd let me borrow it?"

# 37
## FREDDIE & VIOLET

*FREDDIE: My turn to ask a favor.*
*VIOLET: Shoot.*
*FREDDIE: Need to pop out for a bit.*
*VIOLET: When?*
*FREDDIE: 8:00.*
*VIOLET: OK. I'll knock when u can come down. Know*
*when you'll be back?*
*FREDDIE: Not sure.*
*VIOLET: OK. Will leave key under mat in courtyard. If I'm*
*asleep, don't tread on me when u get in!*
*FREDDIE: Haha. OK. Will try to control my clown feet.*

# 38
## FREDDIE & VIOLET

VIOLET: Weird thing happened today . . . .
FREDDIE: ??
VIOLET: A video's going around.
FREDDIE: ??
VIOLET: Of Chris.
FREDDIE: Oh? What's he doing in it?
VIOLET: Well, u can't really see who's filming, but the
camera moves just near the end and u can see this
girl in a hoodie and a massive great big Doberman,
and it's barking and it's got saliva all down its chin,
and Chris is literally crying and begging her to make
it stop.
FREDDIE: Poor Chris. Sounds awful.
VIOLET: Yeah. His life's pretty hellish right now . . . . . .
I'd send u a link to the video but get the feeling uv
already seen it.

FREDDIE: No idea what u mean.

VIOLET: Aha.

FREDDIE: Seriously.

VIOLET: So, it's a coincidence that u told me Scruff's dad is a Doberman? And that u snuck out last night? And that all this happened roughly one day after I told u Chris has been making my life hell?

FREDDIE: Yep.

VIOLET: Well that's a shame. 'Cause if it wasn't, and u did that for me, I'd probably be trying to think of a way to thank u . . .

# 39
## VIOLET

For the third night running, her dad didn't get home until after eight. Violet loved her dad, but he was making everything so hard. Since Freddie had terrorized Chris, her school life was settling into a very undramatic rhythm but now, home was becoming the issue. Although her mum clearly adored Scruff, she was having to walk him morning and evening on her own with her messed-up ankle. Violet volunteered to help, but her mum said not until it got lighter in the evenings. So, she was stuck watching as her mum tried to be Super Mum, and her dad didn't even bother to turn up and spectate.

And Jamie was struggling too. Now, more often than not, he was in bed by the time her dad got home, but he'd try to force himself to stay awake as long as possible, desperate to see him, and then wake in the morning tired and grumpy.

That night, her dad didn't even speak to them. Her mum and Violet were watching TV. Jamie was in bed. And her dad just walked in, chucked his keys on the table in the hall, and went to the bathroom to shower. Violet looked at her mother out of the corner of her eye. She was staring so intently at the television that she wasn't blinking and was chewing the inside of her cheek the way she did when she was trying not to say something.

"You okay?" Violet asked, nudging her mum's arm.

"Hmm? Oh, yes, love. 'Course. Think I'll start getting ready for bed. Turn off the lights before you retire, yes?"

Usually, Violet would have made fun of the way her mum said 'retire' but instead she just nodded and said she would.

Half an hour later, she let Scruff out for his final pee, then went and opened the door to Jamie's room. They'd totally given up trying to convince Scruff to sleep in the kitchen. They had tried. But Scruff had simply cried and howled and whimpered until they'd given in. Obviously, Jamie was thrilled. He loved waking up every morning to find his fluffy best friend asleep on his feet. Violet was beyond happy for her little brother, but she was also a little jealous of how much Scruff loved him. Just once, she would have liked Scruff to choose her bed.

Flopping down in her chair, she took out her phone. So far, her text communication with Freddie had been limited to brief exchanges, never about anything serious. But tonight, like the day with the sludge bucket, she didn't know who else to talk to.

**VIOLET: Think my dad's having an affair.**

**FREDDIE: Whoa. What an opener.**

VIOLET: He's a dick.

FREDDIE: He wouldn't cheat on ur mum.

VIOLET: How do u know?

FREDDIE: They've been married ages.

VIOLET: What's that got to do with anything?

FREDDIE: Does ur mum think he is?

VIOLET: Dunno.

FREDDIE: Not sure I should tell u this . . . . . . . . .

VIOLET: What? What do u know? Have u heard them arguing?

FREDDIE: No. Well, yeah. But that's not it.

VIOLET: What, then?

FREDDIE: I saw him in town just before Xmas. He went into the Ellington.

VIOLET: What's that?

FREDDIE: A hotel.

VIOLET: ??

FREDDIE: He was with a woman.

Violet threw down her phone and hammered on the hatch. "How could you not tell me?" she whisper-yelled as she climbed angrily up through the opening.

Freddie was still clasping his iPod, and he was looking at her as if he she might start throwing things. Something in his face made her calm down, as if he were actually scared of her.

She sat down. "Sorry. But you should have said."

Freddie put the iPod down. "I thought about it, but I didn't know what to say. We were just starting to talk, and I guess I didn't want to ruin it." He paused and held her gaze for a longer than normal amount of time. His eyes were more green than gray tonight, and his hair was shaggy from lying down, sticking up in unruly tufts. "Have I ruined it?"

Violet shook her head. "No. But you need to tell me what you saw."

"Nothing, really. That's mostly why I didn't tell you. All I saw was your dad walking into the hotel with a woman who wasn't your mum. It could have been anyone. A colleague or relative."

Violet swallowed hard. "Did they kiss?"

"No. Nothing like that."

She made Freddie describe the woman but didn't recognize her. Then again, she didn't really know anything about her dad's working life or what he actually did now that he was working for himself. Maybe they were having a meeting. Maybe it was a conference or something. "Okay. Will you do something for me, then?"

"It depends what—"

"I'm not asking you to spy on him or anything. But if you see him again—"

"If I see him again?"

"Just follow him and see what they're doing. If they're, you know," she shuddered at the thought, "getting a room or whatever."

Freddie made a *pffft* sound and said, "I don't know, Violet."

"Please. I need to know. Mum needs to know."

"Okay."

"Okay. Thanks." She paused and pushed her glasses up onto the top of her head. "Listen, I was thinking."

"Uh-oh." He made a "be careful" face.

Violet pinched her eyes at him. "Seriously, I was thinking. Mum and Dad thinking you're my boyfriend is probably the best thing that could have happened."

"It is?" His eyes had brightened. Was he leaning a bit closer?

Violet straightened herself up and tried to sound serious. "Yes. I mean, they think you're working and renting a room somewhere?"

"Uh-huh."

"So, we could tell them you're thinking of moving and you could use this as your postal address. You could sort out your bank account, start looking for a room and a real part-time job and trade school courses."

Something in Freddie's face changed, like a quick dark shadow had moved across it. "I hadn't thought about that."

"Just an idea," she said. But, after that, their conversation dried up and, in the end, she went back to her room wondering what she'd said to make him clam up.

# 40

## FREDDIE

After their conversation about following Violet's dad, Freddie found himself actively not looking at people as they walked past so that he could honestly tell her he'd seen nothing. But then, only a few days later, as if Fate was daring him to get involved, Pete Johnson walked right past Freddie and, just as he had the first time, took a wedge of cash out of the ATM.

Freddie stepped back into the doorway of the coffee shop he'd been walking out of and, through the glass, watched Pete walk away. His heartbeat quickened. He had promised Violet, and if she asked him outright whether he'd seen her father he wasn't sure if he'd be able to lie well enough. Not to her. Strangers, sure; he was great at lying to strangers. But with Violet it was like she saw right into his insides, and even if he didn't want it to the truth came tumbling out.

So he followed Mr. Johnson. He followed him all the way to the Ellington. This time, there was no blonde and Pete went inside alone. Freddie crossed the street and, keeping his head down, entered the hotel lobby. When he looked up, there was no one there. The lobby was totally empty, except for a heavily-made-up receptionist. "Can I help you, sir?" she asked politely.

"Um, I think my friend just came in here? Tall guy, in his forties?"

She frowned. "No, I'm sorry. Just you."

She could have been lying, but Freddie didn't think so. Pete wouldn't have had time to check in and totally disappear in the few seconds it had taken for Freddie to catch him up.

When he stepped back outside it was raining. He was fumbling with the navy-blue umbrella he'd recently bought from Madge's shop when he looked up and noticed the door next to the Ellington's. A small silver plaque read,

*Merlinda Constantine. Grief Counselor.*

Freddie glanced back at the Ellington's door and to where he'd been standing when he'd seen Pete go inside. Could he have gotten it wrong? Holding the umbrella up so it half-obscured his face, he moved so he was standing in front of Merlinda Constantine's window. He peeked through the slatted blinds, and there he was—Pete. The blonde woman Freddie had seen him with had a notepad and a pen and was writing something. Pete was talking, then he put his head in his hands. He was crying.

Freddie looked away, and then he waited across the street, watching the raindrops fall from inside his umbrella, until he saw Pete leave. When Pete was safely around the corner, Freddie folded up the umbrella and tucked it under his arm, then jogged back to Merlinda's door. When he entered her reception area, a bell tinkled, and she came out of the room she'd been in with Pete. She glanced at her watch. "I'm sorry, do we have an appointment?"

"Um. No. I was just wondering whether you have a leaflet. It's for my dad."

Merlinda smiled. She seemed kind. "I don't have a leaflet, I'm afraid, but"—she pointed toward the coffee table that housed magazines and water for those waiting—"there's a business card you could take? It's got my website on there, and—"

"Thanks, that's brilliant."

\* \* \*

That evening, as soon as he heard Violet get in from school, Freddie texted her. *Have news about your dad. Come see me later?* He told her it was good news, but as soon as he'd sent the message, he wondered whether it actually was. Pete clearly wasn't in a very happy place. But, later, when Freddie told Violet what he'd seen and showed her Merlinda's business card, she hugged him and said, "That's it? That's what he's been hiding? A therapist?"

"Seems like it."

Her smile faded as she turned the business card over in her hand. "But why would he hide it? Why wouldn't he just tell Mum?"

Freddie cleared his throat, trying to shift the mem-

ory of his panic attacks and the dark cloud that followed him, even when he was with Violet. "Maybe he's
embarrassed?"

Violet tutted and tossed her hair over her shoulder.
She'd been doing that a lot less recently, but sometimes
she allowed a bit of private school to dictate her man-
nerisms. "Why do guys feel like they have to deal with
emotions on their own? It's ridiculous."

"Do you always talk about your feelings?" Freddie
asked, a little more sharply than he'd meant to.

Violet bit her lower lip. "No. I suppose I don't."

Freddie shrugged at her as if she'd just answered her
own question.

"Okay, so what do we do now? Clearly, Mum needs
to know."

"Does she?"

"Of course. If she knows, she can help him."

Freddie didn't know whether he agreed, but he knew
Violet would do it with or without his help, so he suggested she try to be as subtle as possible. "Why don't
you just leave the business card somewhere your mum
will find it? So it looks like it's slipped out of his pocket?"

"Because he'll probably just deny it."

"Or maybe it'll be the opening he needs to tell her,
without feeling ambushed."

"I don't know."

"Try it. If it doesn't work, we'll think of something else."

# 41

## FREDDIE & VIOLET

VIOLET: It worked.

FREDDIE: The business card?

VIOLET: Yep. They talked for ages last night. Then, really weird, Dad drove me to school and told me in the car.

FREDDIE: About the therapy?

VIOLET: Yeh. It was horrible, actually. He cried.

FREDDIE: What did he say?

VIOLET: Loads of stuff. Sorry for not being around and stuff. He said he's been a real mess since Gran died and he's been trying to fix it all on his own. Apparently, most of the time, in the evenings, he's just been walking around trying to make himself feel better.

FREDDIE: Jeez.

VIOLET: Yeah. I feel so bad for him. And Mum. She must be upset he didn't tell her.

FREDDIE: But they can sort it out now.

VIOLET: FTFB to the rescue!! (again) U need a badge
    or something.
FREDDIE: *blushes*
VIOLET: Seriously. Thanks.
FREDDIE: U know how u can thank me?
VIOLET: Umm . . . . . . a donut?
FREDDIE: Don't make me do anymore spying.
VIOLET: OK.
FREDDIE: And also a donut.
VIOLET: What is it with u and donuts?
FREDDIE: Best. Food. Ever.
VIOLET: Weirdo.

# 42

## FREDDIE

Now that Freddie and Violet were fake boyfriend and girlfriend, and she thought he was a knight in shining, glittery armor because he'd helped with her dad and with the Chris situation, Saturdays were heavenly. He spent them out in the open with her, listening to music or reading together in her room. He'd met both of her parents, and Jamie loved him so much that Violet had to force him out of the room if they wanted to watch something other than *Peppa Pig* on Netflix. By telling Ellie and Pete that Freddie's apartment was pretty sketchy and that the landlord still hadn't gotten around to fixing the hot water or the washing machine, he was even able to shower and clean his clothes.

Everything was so incredibly normal. And they were friends, him and Violet. He was confident of that. But he couldn't work out whether she thought of him as anything more. Every time he thought he'd caught her watching him or sitting a little closer on the floor in front of her bed or lingering as she hugged him good-bye, it was followed by a good few days of her pulling back from him.

They chatted easily, but they didn't talk about his life before he met her, and they didn't talk about his plan for leaving. When she'd mentioned using her parents' address as a way to apply for jobs and apartments and work, he'd frozen. It was exactly what he wanted. It was what he'd been dreaming of, and he had the business card in his pocket, the one belonging to the man from the Christmas fair. But if he tried and it didn't work, then what? He couldn't stay in the attic forever, and he had no back up plan. He had become the archetypal ostrich with its head in the sand.

He didn't see Violet much during the week, which was good because the more normal he felt Saturdays, the worse Sundays became. The hours between waking and going to sleep were torturous. He had his iPod now, which meant he could text Violet, watch Netflix or YouTube, listen to music. But he still itched to be free.

One Sunday near the end of January, it was raining outside, and Freddie had spent most of the morning dozing, his consciousness resting just below the surface of being awake. He became vaguely aware of people talking in Violet's room, and as he focused and the voices became clearer, he realized it was the girl who had uninvited Violet to the fireworks. Way back before they'd first met.

Someone else was there too. Maybe two someone elses.

Violet was saying, "Be right back—you both want hot chocolate?" and then her door closed.

Freddie shuffled closer to the vent above Violet's room. The girls had lowered their voices, but he could hear them. The one he recognized as Aisla laughed and said, "She's totally going to fall for it."

"I dunno," said another.

"Come on, the bet was ten pounds if I can get her to come and another ten if she actually turns up."

"I just don't think she'd be that desperate," said the third, sniggering as she said *desperate*.

Freddie wanted to jump down from the attic and tell them to leave. He picked up his iPod and thought about texting Violet and telling her they were playing some kind of joke on her, but then she returned, and she was chatting so gleefully, so pleased to see her old friends, that he couldn't bear it.

Finally, he heard Aisla say, "So, Vi. It's the cave party next week and, well, I'm really sorry for being such a moron to you. Will you come? Let me make it up?"

There was barely even a pause before Violet said, "Of course I will," and Freddie pictured her hugging Aisla while the other two vipers made faces behind her back. Not for the first time, he was left wondering, Why on earth people are so cruel to one another?

# 43
## FREDDIE & VIOLET

**VIOLET:** Wanna go to a party?

**FREDDIE:** Um . . .

**VIOLET:** Please? My old friend Aisla? She invited me, and I think she's trying to make things up, and I really need to go but I don't have the guts to go alone.

**FREDDIE:** Is it a costume party?

**VIOLET:** Lol. No.

**FREDDIE:** When is it? Need to check calendar.

**VIOLET:** Stop teasing me. Yes or no?

**FREDDIE:** OK. But only 'cause I feel sorry for u.

# 44
## FREDDIE

He should have told her when she asked him to go. He should have replied, *Vi, they're winding you up.* But he didn't, and as they sat side by side on the bus, dangerously close to being normal teenagers going on a normal date, he wondered whether it was because he wanted Violet to show up and prove she was better than them or because the thought of going to a party with her had been too tantalizing to destroy.

Disembarking, Violet informed Freddie that every year Aisla's older sister and her friends set up lights, music, and coolers full of beer in the caves down by the lake at the university. And when Freddie pointed out that it was January and asked if it wasn't a bit cold to be dancing outdoors, she simply rolled her eyes at him as if he was an old man.

The party had been planned long before Violet had left

Briar Ridge and, despite telling Freddie repeatedly that she was only going to be polite, to show her face, to try and keep some form of contact with her old friends, he could tell she was fizzing with anticipation.

The lake was somewhere people like Freddie usually avoided. It was too dark and too isolated to feel comfortable and, descending the slope through the trees, he had to remind himself that tonight he was playing the part of Violet's boyfriend. Not Freddie from the streets.

At the bottom of the slope, Violet tripped and Freddie took her hand to steady her. She didn't take it back, and they walked like that, lighting the way with Violet's phone, until the path became too narrow for them to be side by side. To their right, the lake glistened like a foreboding black mirror. To their left, a sharp incline up into the woods.

"If I didn't know you better, I'd think you'd brought me here to have your wicked way with me," Freddie whispered, immediately tutting at himself for being so cheesy.

Violet chuckled and tossed her hair over her shoulder. She was wearing black leggings and a short animal-print dress with a belt around her middle. She'd curled her hair and re-colored it so the purple was more pronounced. "The night's still young," she replied, playfully elbowing his side. Then, suddenly, it wasn't just them anymore. There were people up ahead and lights through the trees, but no music.

Rounding the bend, Freddie could see clusters of people dancing, waving their arms in the air, bopping their heads and gyrating their hips, but still no music. Then he noticed their headphones. "A silent disco?"

Violet giggled, but before she could respond, a voice

he recognized cut in. "I don't think anyone calls them *discos* anymore, but yeah. If we had speakers we'd be found out before most of us even got here."

"Aisla!" Violet squeaked excitedly, throwing her arms around her friend.

Aisla's looked exactly the way Freddie had pictured her: tanned with dark hair and too-big lips. She was wearing one of those all-in-one suits that he always found ridiculous, and she was exactly the kind of girl Freddie usually avoided. Briefly, she hugged Violet back, maintaining careful eye contact with Freddie. "I don't think we've met?"

Violet shuffled her feet. "Aisla, this is Freddie. My, ah, boyfriend... Are Patts and Daisy here?"

Freddie noted Violet's pause; they hadn't discussed how she would introduce him.

"Boyfriend? Wow, Vi, you didn't say." Aisla was looking at Freddie the way a cat looks at a mouse while deciding whether to play with it or destroy it, and he didn't like the way she'd said *wow*. As if it was remarkable that Violet had found someone who was interested in her.

Freddie vehemently did not want to talk to this girl. Somehow, he felt like she could see straight through him. See all his secrets. But, for Violet, he shrugged it off, tried to remember Freddie with the good hair and the strong jaw, and gave Aisla his most dazzling smile. "Great to meet you," he said warmly, deliberately ignoring Aisla's attempt at shaking hands and, instead, wrapping his arm casually around Violet's shoulders.

Aisla pretended not to care and reached for a nearby ice bucket to offer Freddie a beer.

"No thanks," he replied, "I don't drink."

She raised an eyebrow, instead giving them each a pair of bright blue wireless headphones. "Are you from Violet's new school?"

"Freddie's waiting to start trade school," Violet said, proudly. Not a total lie.

"Cool. Okay, well, I'll find the others and tell them you're here. Have fun..."

And, with that, she was gone.

Turning to Violet, Freddie could see the disappointment etched on her face. "You okay?"

She gave him a fake smile. "Yeah. 'Course."

He paused, waiting for her to continue.

"It's just, I thought we'd...hang out." She buried her face in her hands. "God, that sounds lame."

"No it doesn't. She was your friend."

"*Was.*"

"Look, we're here now. So, let's just. I dunno. Dance?"

"You want to dance?" Violet looked around at the comical movements of the silent dancers surrounding them.

He really didn't. "Yep."

"Okay." She beamed widely, shoving her headphones on and motioning for Freddie to do the same.

Slotting them over his ears, the woods were transformed. The mesmeric beat that now filled his head made everything look different, and as he watched Violet twirl into a person-free space nearby and start waving her arms, he felt, for the first time in such a very long time... happy.

# 45

## VIOLET

Really, the caves weren't caves at all. They were more like arches. But Aisla and her sister had transformed them into some kind of wonderland. Colored lights were strung from the trees. LED candles were balanced here and there on the rocks. And Violet had always wanted to do the headphone thing. She loved that everyone looked ridiculous until you put them on and then you realized that you were all dancing to the same song.

She could tell Freddie was nervous. Apart from New Year's Eve and meeting her mum, this was the most "normal" thing they had done since they'd met. He looked good, though. And he smelled good. He was wearing the gray sweater she'd bought him, and he had just the right amount of stubble. Suddenly, she wasn't sure whether she'd come here to build bridges with Aisla and the girls or to show off her...whatever Freddie was.

As soon as Aisla appeared, though, she knew it had been a mistake to come. The way she looked at Freddie made Violet's blood boil. It was as if he wasn't good enough, as if the only kind of person she'd have been impressed by was one wearing an Armani suit and driving a BMW. She also felt like an idiot. She'd blathered on to Freddie about how amazing it was that Aisla was reaching out to her, how this would be the turning point, how pretty soon things would be back the way they were. And yet, here Aisla was, ghosting her in person.

Freddie tried to make up for it. Despite not drinking, he danced like he didn't care who was watching. And he only had eyes for her. She would never have admitted it to him, but when Aisla had stalked up to them wearing her plunging jumpsuit and massive heels, all pouty and long haired and gorgeous, Violet had studied Freddie's expression so closely she'd felt like she'd been about to burn holes into his face. But he hadn't shown even the smallest glimmer of interest and, now, he was well and truly lost in Violet's company.

As they danced, they circled closer and closer to each other until, finally, they began to touch. His hand on her waist, hers on his shoulder, then the small of his back, his fingers on her face, tucking her hair behind her ear, like in the movies, his lips on hers.

Freddie was kissing her, and it was perfect. It was exactly how she'd pictured it so many times when they were sitting in her room talking and reading and not touching. Why hadn't she allowed this to happen sooner? They should have been doing this all along, from the beginning.

When they finally broke apart, they stared at each other for a moment. Violet wished they were alone. Wished all these people would go away, stop looking at them. Why did she feel like they were being looked at? Taking her eyes away from Freddie's, Violet looked around and realized exactly why: Aisla, Patti, Daisy, and a cluster of others were very obviously laughing at her.

Quickly, she removed her headphones. She wasn't sure whether she was angry they were laughing, angry at everything that had happened since she'd left Briar Ridge, or angry that they'd ruined her perfect moment with Freddie. Whatever the reason, the two cans of lager she'd forced herself to drink were sloshing through her veins and making her feel brave, so she stalked over to them, shoved her face so close to Aisla's that she could smell the berry flavor of her lip gloss, and shouted, "When did you become such an epic bitch?!"

For a second, Aisla looked totally taken aback. But then she rallied. "Bitch?!" She shoved Violet, hard, in the chest. Violet stepped back and stumbled, falling flat on her backside.

Freddie was at her side, scooping her up, but Aisla wasn't done.

"You need to take a look at yourself, Violet. You're pathetic. Still hanging about here when we've tried to get rid of you. And we've all heard what you've been up to at Arnhurst. Slutting it up with anyone who'll have you. It's sad, really. But I guess it just proves what we knew all along. You were always the hanger on. The odd one out. Well now maybe you'll leave us alone and we'll never have to see your skinny, disgusting face ever again." Her words were pure venom. Even the gaggle of girls flanking her looked uncomfortable.

Violet was shaking; she didn't know what to say or do. Tears were biting at the backs of her eyes, and she was almost certain she'd sprained her ankle. She felt Freddie squeeze her waist and start to steer her away. "Don't say anything. Don't give them the satisfaction. They're not worth it."

# 46

## FREDDIE

Violet was drunk, sobbing, and limping as they made their way back by the lake. Freddie practically had to carry her up the slope and then finally, at what she obviously considered a safe distance away from Aisla, she stopped.

"I'm so sorry," she said. "I should never have made us come."

Freddie brushed a few tear-sodden strands of hair away from her cheeks. "This isn't your fault."

"Of course, it is. I knew it was a bad idea. I don't even know why I came. What was I trying to prove?"

"Honestly, Vi. Stop. If it's anyone's fault, it's mine. I should have told you..." He let the sentence fade away, hoping perhaps she hadn't noticed, that she wouldn't try to fill in the blank.

"Told me what? Do you know something? What do

you know?" Her speech was slurred, and she was obviously struggling to focus on his face. He didn't want to have this conversation now. He didn't want to have it at all, but especially not like this.

"Nothing, I just—"

"Freddie, don't lie to me."

"I heard them talking, in your room."

Violet looked at him expectantly.

"It was a bet. They had a bet about whether you'd come. Whether you'd have the nerve to show up."

"A bet? This was a bet? And you knew?"

Freddie hung his head. There was no way out of it. No way that she wouldn't see this as a betrayal. He wanted to say something, wanted to conjure some magic words to make her understand, but he couldn't think of any, and the more Violet shouted the more he shrank back. He had never liked confrontation but since everything with his dad, he now couldn't bare it at all.

"You knew that they invited me here to make fun of me? And you didn't tell me?"

"I wanted you to show them that you're better than them, to come here and be you and prove that you don't need them anymore."

"But that wasn't your decision to make." Her voice had softened, which almost made him feel worse.

"I know. I'm sorry."

"What else do you know? What other secrets have you been listening to? First my dad, and now this? Is this what you do? You skulk around in our house, listening for information you can use to manipulate us? Is this all some kind of sick, twisted game?"

Freddie could feel his mouth opening and closing, but

he still couldn't find the right words.

"I shouldn't be surprised, should I, really? I mean what kind of idiot finds a boy living in her attic and doesn't call the police? Just acts as if it's totally normal. It's stupid. *I'm* stupid."

"No, you're not, you're kind—"

"Yes, I am! And I trusted you. Out of everyone in my life, you were the one I trusted." She was crying again. The tears were coming thick and fast, and she was taking deep, gasping breaths between her words. "I thought you were the one person who would never lie to me."

"I didn't—"

"Lying by omission is still lying, Freddie. What other secrets are you hiding? What other lies? I've never asked you about your past. I've never asked you about any of it. I just trusted you."

"I've never lied to you about anything, Vi. I promise."

"Problem is, it seems you've got a funny definition of lying." She took a step back from him, distancing herself, taking a deep breath as if she was preparing for what she was about to say.

Freddie felt the way he'd felt when he encountered Janet on the street, like he was some kind of alien, some untouchable thing she didn't want to be anywhere near.

"I want you to leave. I never want to see you again."

There it was. The sentence he'd been expecting ever since they met. It could have been the alcohol talking, but in his experience, alcohol just gave people the bravado to say what they really felt.

"I'll put your things in the courtyard, but I don't want to see you. Whatever this is—it's over."

Freddie knew he should say something. He knew he

shouldn't just let her walk away. But what could he say? She was right. There was so much he'd never told her. So much he couldn't ever say to her. Briefly, an alternative timeline flashed through his mind. One in which he told her everything, where it all came tumbling out and he told her about his mum and his dad and the drinking and Amy and Janet and losing the house and all of it. Every horrible, awful detail. But then he saw the way it would really go: he would say all of those things, and she would realize he was a monster. To be honest, that was probably the way it was heading anyway. So, maybe it was better it ended like this—an argument in the woods, and then he'd be gone.

Violet was walking away. She wasn't looking back. She was still limping and swaying a little, but there was purpose in her walk. Freddie hated the thought of her going home alone in the dark. But what could he do? He couldn't follow her. What would that make him? A stalker as well as a voyeur. So he just stayed rooted to the spot and watched her leave. Watched her fade into the distance just like he'd watched the Johnsons' car all those months ago.

He was trying to quash the familiar feeling of dread at the long cold hours ahead when he heard movement in the bushes behind him. He turned to see Aisla stumbling up the slope in her high heels. She was alone, and he wondered briefly whether she'd come to see if Violet was okay. If she had, she didn't give any impression of it. She straightened herself up and stared at him with the same stony eyes she'd had when they first met.

"She's left you, has she? I'm not surprised."

Freddie sighed and started to walk away, but then he

stopped and turned back. "Can I ask you something?"

Aisla cocked her head and widened her eyes as if to say, *Okay, I dare you.*

"Does it make you feel good?"

She tensed her jaw and ran her tongue along her teeth.

"Treating people the way you do—does it make you feel good? Does it help you forget whatever horrible shit is going on in your life?"

Her face softened at that.

"'Cause the thing is, Aisla, life is so much bigger than you. Everyone has stuff going on, but I promise you that in a year, two years, ten years, you're going to look back and you're going to hate the way you behaved in this moment."

Aisla rolled her eyes. "Thanks, Grandad."

# 47
## VIOLET

At home, lying in bed and staring at the ceiling, Violet remained angry. She didn't regret telling Freddie to leave. In fact, it was all she could do to stop herself going up to the attic right then and there and tossing out all his things. He had lied to her. She'd trusted him, and he lied. And, really, she only had herself to blame.

She was still angry when she woke up. Something tugged unpleasantly at her insides when she gathered up his sleeping bag and backpack, but she ignored it and shoved them out into the courtyard. She contemplated looking through the bag, but what would be the point? She didn't care who he was or what he did next. She just wanted him gone.

After pulling her curtains shut, she buried herself under her duvet and went back to sleep. At various intervals, her mum and Jamie tried to rouse her, but she simply grunted and embroiled herself tighter in her quilt, concentrating on thinking about nothing.

As the day wore on, however, she had to try harder and harder not to wonder where Freddie had slept last night or where he was now. Once or twice, she peeped out to see whether he'd come for his belongings, but they were still there by the wall at the back.

Sometime in the afternoon, the doorbell rang, and her mum called, "Vi, you've got a visitor."

"Tell Freddie I don't want to see him!" Violet shouted, feeling her voice wobble.

A tap on the door.

"Mum, seriously..."

Her mum poked her head tentatively into the room, smiling. "It's not Freddie. It's Aisla, love."

Violet threw off her duvet and tried to smooth her bedhead, but before she could even reach halfway presentable, Aisla flounced in.

Her mum shut the door and left them to it.

Neither of them spoke. Then, crossing her arms in front of her chest, Violet eventually said, "If you've come for round two, I'm not in the mood."

Aisla looked at her feet. "I didn't."

"Right. So?"

Aisla walked past Violet and perched in the hanging egg chair, then stood up again and moved over toward the desk. Not meeting Violet's eyes, she said curtly, "I came to apologize, okay? I don't want to be friends anymore, but I shouldn't have been such a bitch about it. I'm sorry."

Violet raised an eyebrow.

Aisla looked at her but then quickly looked away

again. "I miss you and I hate it, and I'm no good at long distance. I know that's crap of me, but it's true. If we don't see each other every day it won't work. So, I guess I did what I did because it made it not hurt so much. It's twisted. I know. But I can't handle it, and that's that."

Violet had never known Aisla to drop her barriers, even a little. She wanted to hug her. But that wasn't the point of this. The point was that their friendship was over. "Okay."

"Maybe in the future...or whatever."

Violet nodded slowly. Then, as Aisla was about to leave, she said, "Who made you come? Daisy or Patts?"

Aisla stopped and laughed a little. "It was your boyfriend, actually."

"Freddie?"

"I guess you two had a fight? He was on his own. Gave me some kernels of wisdom. Something about Future Me hating the way I behaved and how everyone has stuff to deal with and I'm nothing special... He was right."

Violet glanced out to the courtyard. Every ounce of anger she felt was suddenly and miraculously gone. She'd done exactly what Aisla had, hadn't she? Said horrible things and made herself angry so that Freddie's untruth wouldn't hurt so much.

"Whatever you fought about, I'd let it go, Vi. He seems really nice." For a second, Aisla smiled at her the way she used to, and Violet felt as if they were mere moments away from curling up with hot chocolate and Netflix and those ridiculous unicorn onesies they'd bought last Christmas and finally being back to normal. But then the smile was gone. And so was she.

Violet remained on the edge of her bed. She looked up at the ceiling and out at the courtyard. Then she checked her phone, despite knowing Freddie couldn't have texted her. *"I never want to see you again,"* she had told him. *Never.*

They had spoken so little of his life before he came to the Johnsons'. Where would he go? Where had he slept last night? A sickening tightness gripped her chest. She'd been so angry. She'd painted over every good thing Freddie had done for her and for her family and forced him back onto the street—probably the worst thing she could ever have done to him.

She pictured him huddled in a doorway. Or maybe he'd waited until the end of the party and snuck back to the caves to sleep. He didn't even have a jacket. She'd told him not to bother taking one because she hadn't wanted to turn up looking like two people who'd been walking their dog. She hadn't wanted to give Aisla and the others any ammunition. How ridiculous that seemed now.

Finally forcing herself to move, she retrieved Freddie's things from the corner of the courtyard. She stared at them for a moment, feeling the weight of his backpack in her hand—barely anything, and yet that was everything he owned.

She had never looked through his things. Never snuck into the attic when he was out and tried to find out about his life or his past. But how else could she find him? Instantly, she caved and pulled on the drawstring, peering in as though something might jump out and bite her.

She didn't empty it all onto the floor—that felt wrong. Instead, she reached inside and felt for his wallet. He hadn't taken it to the party, he'd just put a ten-pound note from his stash into his pocket. Ten pounds, that was all he had. Her fingers brushed against his crumpled suit, a book, a water bottle, some socks, and then she found it.

Inside, Freddie had no bank cards. Just two five-pound notes. She opened the zip where the coins should be kept. No coins, but there was a driving license. Frederick Samuel Miller. Freddie had a name. And an address below the name: 12 All Saints Road, Olton. She burned it into her memory, even though it felt like a betrayal. Behind the license was a business card:

*Pay What You Can Kitchen*
*St. Barnabas Community Center, Newton*
*Open: Tuesday, Thursday, Saturday, and Sunday*
*9:00 a.m.–4:00 p.m.*

\* \* \*

By the time she reached the community center, it was four-thirty and the doors were locked. She tried the handle three times and then just stood, staring, wondering if maybe she came back on Monday, camped out for the day, she'd find him.

Then the door opened. A short haired, dumpy-looking girl in a puffy jacket and velvet joggers appeared, gave her the briefest of glances, and then set about bringing in the sandwich board sign that listed the kitchen's open hours outside.

Violet remained where she was, and eventually, the girl said, "Can I help you?"

"I'm...ah...I'm looking for someone."

The girl folded her arms across her chest. "Yeah?"

Violet stepped forward, brandishing her phone with its background picture of her and Freddie and Jamie pulling stupid faces. "His name's—"

"Freddie," the girl interjected. She looked Violet up and down but didn't invite her inside. "You're the one he's been staying with?"

He'd told someone about her? "Yes. But he left. I didn't know where to look..." She trailed off, aware that she sounded as though she barely knew him at all.

The girl chewed her lip, clearly trying to decide whether Violet deserved her help. "Have you tried the church?"

Violet looked around, as if a church might spring up somewhere behind her.

"The one on North Street. We used to go there a lot."

She said *we*, so she and Freddie had been what? Friends? More than friends? "Thank you, thanks so much. I'll try it now. But if you see him—"

"I'll tell him you were here."

"My name's Violet."

"Okay."

"And tell him...tell him I didn't mean it?"

The girl unfolded her arms and reached for the door handle. Then turned back. "Freddie's one of the good ones. So, if you're helping him, then help him. But don't make him some kind of pet project, then drop him when it suits you. 'Cause that'll make it all a hundred times worse. Okay?"

"Okay."

# 48

## FREDDIE

After he walked away from Aisla, Freddie headed for the bus stop. But the one in the opposite direction to Violet's. He had a ten-pound note in his pocket and, for the first time in so many months, he found himself wondering how long he would have to stretch out his meager amount of money for.

He didn't want to waste it on the bus and, besides, the adult shelter—the only one left since the youth shelter had closed—would be full by now so there was no point trying to make it. So, he walked. In his too-big, posh shoes he walked all the way into town.

As he walked, he thought about that night on Walnut Avenue. About what would have happened if he had just left the notebook where it had been on the doorstep, if he hadn't gone inside, if he hadn't met Violet.

What was the old saying? "It's better to have loved

and lost than never to have loved at all." But was it? If he had carried on as he was. If he hadn't spent the last three months living with Violet, in her house, albeit in the attic. If he hadn't been given a glimpse of how different his life could be, would he have felt like this? Like he was cracking at the edges, breaking in half.

For once, though, Freddie wasn't angry with himself; he was disappointed. He had been careful from the very beginning, never to let himself get too comfortable. He'd known that as soon as he relaxed, took it for granted, it would all come tumbling down. And that was exactly what had happened. In that moment, dancing with Violet, he had felt like her boyfriend, like normal Freddie. He had felt like he used to but better because he was with Violet, and before he had never had anyone as remotely as good as her in his life. He had had that moment of utter happiness—and then it had disintegrated. Every ounce of it. Gone.

And now he was back to where he'd started.

As he walked, he tried to think about whether Violet had really meant the things she said. Maybe she would text him and say sorry and ask him to come home. But even if she did, Freddie knew that he couldn't go back.

The only thing that made him contemplate it was picturing his photograph of Amy, tucked inside the over-read copy of *The Tiger Who Came to Tea* that he kept buried at the bottom of his bag. She had loved that story. On the nights when his dad and Janet had gone out and Freddie had tucked her in to bed, she had made him read it again and again and again until her eyes had finally drooped and she'd whispered, "Gobblers."

She'd gotten that from him—gobblers—and he'd gotten it from his mum. Her mum had said it every night, right from when he was small, and it wasn't until not long before she died that he'd finally asked her what it meant.

She had laughed, then. The first real laugh he'd heard from her in weeks. Her eyes had creased at the edges and sparkled the way they always used to. "Oh, my love," she had said, breathlessly. "All these years, that's what you thought I was saying to you? 'Gobblers'..."

Freddie had laughed back, despite not knowing what he was laughing at, and she had taken his hand and squeezed it. "Freddie, darling boy, it's not 'gobblers', it's 'God bless'."

When it had come to the day, the one when she had been no longer opening her eyes and they'd known it was time, Freddie had whispered that to her again and again and again. And then, and he knew his dad never believed him when he told him, just before it happened, she'd whispered back, "Gobblers."

He couldn't remember now how he'd come to share it with Amy. Had he told her the story? Or had he just started saying it?

* * *

Usually, in the days before Violet, Freddie would have gone to an all-night café and tried to eke out these hours. But tonight, he needed to do something different. He didn't want to admit that this was it—the start of his old routine all over again. So, he did what he had sworn to himself he would never do—he went to a bar.

The one he chose was similar to the one he'd used to drag his dad out of at two in the morning. Down a side street, peeling wallpaper, dark lighting, disgusting restrooms, loud music, and cheap shots. He had intended to just sit. Let the noise drown out his thoughts. But then he found himself standing at the bar and a man next to him said in a slurred voice, "Man, you look like you need a drink. Let me..."

Freddie meant to say, "No," but, instead, heard himself saying, "Thanks." And before he could really think about it, a double whiskey, no ice, no mixer, was placed sharply in front of him. Freddie swilled it around in the glass. It was his dad's drink. To stop the remembering, he swigged it back and then requested another. After the second drink, Freddie looked at the remaining cash in his palm and asked the bartender, "How many more can I get with this?"

"I'm feeling generous: I'll do you three for two."

Freddie nodded and, as the drinks were lined up in front of him, the man beside him said, "That's the way to do it mate. Wash it allll awaaaayyy."

\* \* \*

The next morning, early, Freddie woke with a hammering pain in his right temple. He looked up. He wasn't outside, and he wasn't in the attic. He looked around and spotted his friend from the bar, slumped in a chair in the corner of what appeared to be a grimy apartment, wearing just his underwear and cradling a half-full takeout pizza box.

Freddie raised his hand to his head and winced, realizing that the pain wasn't coming from a hangover but from some kind of injury. He got up and stumbled to the kitchen sink. On a tiny shelf above it, there was a cracked shaving mirror. Freddie peered into it and saw that his hair was matted and caked in blood from a cut above his right eyebrow.

He walked over to the man from the bar and shook his shoulder. The man grunted and rolled over, sending the pizza box sliding to the floor. Freddie looked at it longingly, but he couldn't bring himself to take it.

The apartment wasn't far from the main street or the bar, and as Freddie stumbled on autopilot toward Starbucks, he reminded himself that this was precisely why he didn't drink. It was bad enough under normal circumstances. But for people like him, it made you vulnerable. That man from the bar could have been anyone, he could have murdered Freddie in his sleep and Freddie wouldn't have been able to do a thing about it.

Vaguely, he remembered throwing up in the toilet at the bar and the man saying, "Let it all out, fella, let it all out." But then the memories stopped; he had no idea how he'd cut his forehead. It could have been from anything or anyone. They could have robbed somewhere, gotten into a fight, hurt someone. Freddie felt sick at the thought of it.

When he reached Starbucks, he looked at his reflection in the window and contemplated asking someone to buy him a coffee. But who would buy that guy a coffee? He was spiraling, and he could feel it. A darkness inhabited the pit of his stomach. It lurked over his shoulder and somewhere below his feet, and if he was ever teetering on the edge, the one thing guaranteed to send him over was alcohol. It amplified the self-doubt and the self-loathing and made it so loud Freddie could barely think. There was only one place he could go.

He reached the church at ten-thirty, just after their morning service. At the back, he lit a candle even though he had no money to put into the donations box, and then he slipped into a pew a few rows from the front. He breathed in slowly through his nose and out through his mouth and looked up at the stained-glass window.

He tried to empty his mind and tried not to remember all the times he'd come here before. He tried not to think about Violet and what she'd say if she saw him the way he'd been last night. He tried not to berate himself for being exactly the opposite of what he always wanted to be when he was with her. Tried not to think of how disappointed his mum and Amy would be if they saw him like this...

Eventually, a sense of calm trickled through him. Not because he was in a place of God and not because he thought God was looking after him because, let's face it, what had God done for him so far? But because that's what always happened when he was in a church, any church. It was like the buildings themselves held the memories of people's prayer, people's faith, and they seeped into his skin and into his bones and made him feel better. Not better forever, but better for the moments he sat there. And, for those moments, not alone either.

So, Freddie sat in the church, and he kept on sitting. He sat through the afternoon service, and when the vicar approached him and asked if he was all right, he replied, "Can I stay?"

* * *

It was getting dark. Freddie was sitting with his head in his hands and his eyes closed, halfway between being asleep and awake, when he felt a hand on his shoulder.

"I didn't know you were religious." It was Violet's voice, and Freddie opened his eyes to see a shimmering version of her sitting beside him. This kind of thing had happened before. After his mum had died, he used to see her all the time—in the kitchen, the street, at the end of his bed. He put his head back into his hands.

"Freddie, are you okay?" This time, Violet was touching his leg, and when he looked up, she suddenly came into focus.

"It's you."

"Yes. It's me."

What must she have thought of him? "How did you find me?"

She pursed her lips, and he heard her teeth chattering together the way they did when she was nervous. "I looked in your wallet. I found the card for the Kitchen and—"

"Gina," he said.

"Is that her name? It seems like you two are good friends. She obviously cares about you a lot."

If Violet was trying to find out whether Gina had ever been more than a friend, Freddie didn't give her an answer. Mainly because he wasn't really sure what he and Gina were. He always knew she liked him, and he liked her too, just not like that.

"Freddie, I'm sorry for what I said. I didn't mean any of it."

He gave her a weary smile. "Yeah. You did."

"Okay, well maybe I meant them in the moment. Maybe I thought I meant them, but I didn't... What I said about not knowing who you are, that was ridiculous. Of course, I know you—"

"No, Vi. You don't. How could you?" He shuffled away from her and looked down at his hands, which were clasped so tightly in his lap that his knuckles were turning white. "You should have thrown me out the second you met me. All I bring is darkness." He took a deep breath. "It's better this way."

Violet grabbed one of his hands and ducked to meet his eyes, forcing him to look at her. She smiled. "You don't bring darkness. That's nonsense. Look at what you did for Jamie and for me—you *saved* me from Chris Parker—and you helped me with Mum and Dad, and," she sighed, "Freddie, just come home. Come home, have a shower and something to eat, and we'll talk about it."

"I can't."

"Of course, you can. Just come with me."

"Violet, I can't. I can't do it anymore. I can't keep lying to people. Every day I dress up in a suit and I lie to people to get them to give me money. I lie to your mum and dad every time I see them, and I make you lie to them. And, okay, I haven't lied to you, but there are so many things I haven't told you, things I can't ever tell you..."

"Okay, but I have a plan. A real plan. Here..." Violet reached behind her, and when she turned back she was grinning. "It's a prospectus from the trade school, and forms. They give scholarships for some of their courses. I'll help you apply."

Freddie's head was spinning, and he was dangerously close to being swept up in her daydream. Her eyes were bright and shiny, waiting for him to tell her she'd fixed it all. Freddie stood up and walked toward the lectern at the front of the church. He was crying and he didn't want her to see, but he couldn't stop. They weren't just tears; they were sobs. Great, heaving, ugly sobs that made his body shake and his nose start to run. He sat down on the steps in front of the stained-glass window.

Violet crouched in front of him and reached up her hands to cradle his face. "Come home, Freddie."

# 49

## VIOLET

They didn't speak on the journey home. It had only been one night, but he looked thinner already and gray around the edges. His eyes were different too. A little bloodshot, yes, but that wasn't what worried her. It was their light—it was missing. She tried not to keep looking at the blood in his hair. What on earth had happened to him? What had she done?

When they reached Walnut Avenue, she told him to just head for the bathroom when they walked in and let her do the talking. He nodded, and when she opened the front door, after checking her parents were in the living room, he moved quickly down the hall.

"Freddie's here. He's taking a shower," she called.

"Okay, love," her mum called back.

"Freddie, remind me and I'll come look at that shower..." her dad shouted, as though he would actually have a clue what to do in order to fix it.

With Freddie and his bloody forehead safely locked in the bathroom, Violet grabbed his bag from where she'd hidden it under her bed. She tapped lightly on the door, and he opened it, just a crack. She held out the bag, and he took it. "Be out in a minute."

She waited, then waited some more, and when the shower still hadn't started after five minutes of her standing there, she pressed her ear to the door, reminding herself that Freddie had listened to them every single day, so it couldn't really have been that bad of her, could it?

At first, she heard nothing. So much nothing that she wondered whether he'd escaped out of the window. But then, she heard him crying. He had cried in the church. Big, loud, ugly cries that made his face red and his eyes startlingly green, but this was different. This was the silent, desperate cry of someone who didn't want anyone to hear them.

Wrapping her arms around herself, Violet headed for the living room and perched in the armchair near the window. Her mum looked over at her. "All right, Vi?"

"Mm, yep," she replied, attempting a smile.

"Freddie still in the bathroom?" her dad asked, looking behind him toward the hall as though Freddie might be lurking there.

"Yeah, not feeling great, I think."

Her mum gave a sympathetic nod, and her dad nodded. "Tea, El?"

"Ooh, yes, please."

For once, they were being nice to each other, and Violet found it disconcerting. They'd had a date night last night, maybe that was why. Her mum was even sitting with her legs across her dad's lap, the way she'd used to. Really, it was the tiniest of gestures, but Violet felt as if she should look away. Her dad gently stood up and went to the kitchen. Then suddenly Freddie was there, wet haired and fresh, but with a very obvious cut above his eyebrow. How would they explain this one?

Her mum noticed it instantly. "Oh, Freddie," she said, standing and fussing. "What happened?"

Freddie winced at her touch, and Violet wasn't sure whether it was because it hurt or because he hadn't expected it.

"Didn't I tell you?" Violet asked, thinking as she was speaking. "Someone knocked into him at Aisla's stupid headphone party."

"Oh?" Her mum wasn't convinced.

Freddie attempted a sort of half-chuckle, half-laugh and shook his hair so it fell over his face. "You should see the other guy," he quipped.

\* \* \*

They spent the next half hour drinking tea and watching a rerun of *Pointless* with her parents—Freddie on one side of the room, on the floor with his legs stretched out and his back to the footstool, and her on the other. He smiled the way he always did and answered almost all the questions right, the way he always did, but when he thought no one was watching the smile disappeared and he looked on the verge of getting up and running away.

Eventually, her mum went to run a bath and her dad

locked himself away in his study. Violet checked on Jamie, then joined Freddie in her room. She put on their favorite playlist and sat beside him on the bed. "Something's different, isn't it?" she asked, almost reaching for his hand but then letting her fingers linger on the duvet between them.

"Different?"

"Between us. It feels...strange."

Freddie shook his head, sighed, then twisted his torso so that he was, finally, looking at her properly. "I'm...embarrassed," he said. "You've seen me now, Vi. The real me. The one who doesn't shower or sleep. The one who wears the same clothes three days in a row or longer. The one who feels, just...helpless. And, I guess, I hoped you wouldn't ever have to see that version of me."

He was looking at her with big, sad, watery eyes. But Violet couldn't help it; she laughed.

Freddie blinked and sat up a little straighter.

"I'm sorry," she said, stifling the laugh. "It's just that you basically just described *every* teenage boy on the planet."

Freddie grimaced, and Violet prodded him in the ribs.

"Come on, it's not that bad. We had a stupid fight. But you're back now. I'm not making light of it all, I promise. But you can't let yourself start thinking like this, or it'll just get worse." She tucked her head under his chin and rested it on the spot near his collarbone. He smelled like Freddie again. "We'll fix it. All of it. Now that you're back."

Finally, he wrapped his arm around her, and she felt his muscles begin to un-tense.

"I have an idea—wait there."

She left him sitting on the bed and padded quickly to her parents' bathroom. "Mum?"

She didn't hear her mother's sigh, but she felt it even from behind the door. "Yes, Violet..."

"Can I come in? I need to ask you something."

A pause. Then, "Okay, yep. Come in."

Her mum was lying in the dark, candles dotted around the room, bubbles up to her chin. She didn't sit up, just rolled her head in Violet's direction and opened one eye. "What is it, Vi?"

Violet sat down on the closed toilet seat and twisted her fingers in her lap, trying to think of the optimum phrasing for what she was about to say. "The thing is, Freddie's having a tough time at the moment. I know it sounds strange, but he's lonely and I'm worried he's getting a bit depressed and so I was wondering if he could stay here tonight?"

There. The question was out. She glanced sideways at her mum, who was now sitting up with her arms folded on her knees. "On the sofa?"

"Well, I was hoping..."

"Violet, there is no way your father would agree to you having a boyfriend stay in your room. He'd probably be okay with a cot in the living room, but—"

"Mum. Please." Violet was looking her in the eyes now, begging silently for her to see how important this was.

Her mum sighed and narrowed her eyes. "If it was up to me, I might consider it—"

"We're not having sex," Violet blurted. "It's not about that, and even if it was, if we were that desperate, we wouldn't need him to sleep over to do it.

Sleeping is just about sleeping. I promise, Mum. He just needs me tonight."

"All right, let me think about it."

Violet started to smile.

"I'm not saying yes. I'm saying I'll think about it."

"Okay. Thanks, Mum. Thanks."

\* \* \*

About an hour later, her mum knocked on Violet's door, in her towel, and whispered, "One night. And *don't* tell your father."

# 50
## FREDDIE

Freddie with the strong jaw, Freddie from before the streets, would have jumped through the roof at the thought of sharing a bed with a girl like Violet Johnson. But, lying in a real bed for the first time in nearly two years, Freddie was asleep before he even had chance to say goodnight.

# 51
## VIOLET

"Freddie, everything's going to be okay." She snuggled closer to his warm, bony torso and draped her arm across his chest. "And. I was wondering..." She paused, jigging her teeth together nervously. "Do you want to be my real boyfriend now?"

Silence.

"Freddie?"

But Freddie was already asleep.

# 52
## VIOLET

Before Freddie woke up, Violet tapped on the door to her dad's study and he told her to come in. He was sitting at his desk, laptop open, printer printing, paperwork spread out in what she assumed was organized chaos. He pushed his glasses on top of his head and spun his chair to face her.

"You okay, Vi?"

She sat down cross-legged on the floor and picked at a hole in her sock. "Dad?"

"Mmm?"

"Can I ask you something?"

"We're not getting another dog—"

Violet laughed. "No. Not that kind of something. I, um, I wanted to ask about your therapy."

Her dad sat up and shuffled in his chair.

"It's just—I think Freddie's having a hard time. You

know his mum died when he was little? Well, I don't think he's really ever dealt with it, and..." She trailed off; she wasn't really sure what she was asking.

"You think Freddie would benefit from seeing a therapist?"

"Probably. But he couldn't afford it."

Her dad scratched his chin. "Okay. Well, if he sees his doctor, they might be able to... Not what you're after?"

Violet shook her head. "That'll take ages. I need to know how I can help him now."

"Right." Her dad's neck was reddening. He tugged at the collar of his sweater, then got up from his chair and sat on the floor beside her. "I think the best thing you can do, Vi, is to listen."

"But what if he doesn't want to talk?"

"Just give him time. The biggest thing that helped me wasn't necessarily the fact that Merlinda had lots of qualifications. It was more just having a safe place to talk about my feelings." He rolled his eyes at himself. "You know us guys aren't very good at that sometimes."

"A safe place?"

"Yes. Someone impartial you can talk to, so you don't worry about being judged or upsetting anyone else."

Violet nodded. She had an idea. "Thanks, Dad, that's really helpful."

"Is it?" Her dad seemed surprised.

"Yeah." She gave him a brief but firm hug. "Yeah, really helpful."

# 53

## FREDDIE

Freddie slept in Violet's bed until ten-thirty the next morning. He would probably have slept the entire day, but she woke him with coffee and a bacon sandwich, sitting next to him with one leg tucked underneath her. He smiled, even though he still felt empty and raw.

"Eat up," she said. "You'll soon feel better."

How could he explain to her that he probably wouldn't? He'd been here before. Once the grayness had crept in, it was so exhaustingly hard to push it away again.

"I've had an idea." Violet walked over to her bookcase, took down a black leather notebook and waved it at him. "I haven't written in it yet. I have a bit of a phobia of messing up beautiful stationery." She sat back down and placed it purposefully between them. "Okay, so, before Mum and Dad moved me to Briar Ridge—"

"Your private school?"

"Mm-hmm. Before they moved me there, I was a brat. I don't really know why. I was just so full of...feelings. I was hanging out with these girls who were all very 'deep' and full of 'feelings' too, and we were, well, we were stupid. We skipped school. Smoked. Snuck out in the middle of the night to hang out in cars with not very nice boys. It was all very clichéd and not at all original.

"I made Mum's life hell, and then one day she started this thing—she said to me that she knew it was hard to talk about stuff sometimes, especially with people you're close to. So, she gave me this diary, and she said that if there was anything I wanted to tell her or ask her or get out in the open, I could write it down and leave the diary on my bed. Each morning, she'd collect it and read it and write me a reply. Sometimes she'd ask me stuff back, but I didn't have to answer if I didn't want to, and we'd never talk about it in person. Not unless I instigated it."

Freddie smiled. He'd always convinced himself that if his mum had been alive and they had been at home together through his worst teenage years, he'd have been an angel. He imagined her giving him advice about girls, watching movies together in the evenings, messing about with a football in the park. In reality, however, he knew that if she'd been alive, he wouldn't have appreciated her; he'd have been a filthy, rude, grunting boy. She would have loved the diary idea. "That's really nice," he said.

"Yeah. It was. I was still a brat, but we got each other a bit more, I think."

"Do you still do it?"

"We talk in person now, mostly. If I'm not being cagey. But the reason I'm telling you is because I thought..." She paused, looking down at the cover of the notebook and tapping it lightly with her fingernail. "I thought maybe me and you could try it?"

Immediately, Freddie's muscles tensed. "I don't know, Violet—"

"Just hear me out—I think it could help. I could write stuff to you, and you could write stuff to me. No judgments. No talking or texting about it. It would just be here, in the book. A totally safe place to, I dunno, exorcise your demons."

She was looking at him with big expectant eyes. She was trying to help him. Maybe he should let her. "Okay. I'll try."

"You will?" she seemed genuinely surprised.

Freddie nodded.

Violet reached for his coffee cup and his empty plate, put them on the floor, then snuggled in beside him and took hold of his hand. "Everything's going to be okay."

\* \* \*

They spent the afternoon together, watching back-to-back episodes of *Game of Thrones*, then had dinner with Ellie, Pete, and Jamie. After dinner, he left through the front door, walked across the road and down to the bus stop, then back to the alley behind Violet's courtyard. The knotted rope of sheets was already there, and he levered himself over the wall. Inside, they stood beside the bed and Violet handed him the notebook. "Just write what you need to write. No judgments. Remember?"

He hugged her. Normally, he'd have hugged her for more moments than he should have because he was thinking about kissing her or running his fingers down her back and her arms and across her stomach. But tonight, it was because he was scared to let go. Eventually, Violet pulled away and glanced at her door. "You'd better go. Sorry."

He told her it was okay, then heaved himself back up through the hatch. Sitting on his sleeping bag, he opened the notebook and started writing. He didn't think, he just wrote and wrote and kept writing until his hand cramped up and his words became less and less legible. The next morning, he left it on Violet's bed after she went to school. Then, instead of putting on his suit and hustling, he returned to the attic and slept.

# 54
## VIOLET

Violet hadn't expected Freddie to write anything, but he had filled two pages.

*My mum was beautiful. I remember her having big cheeks, big eyes, and a big smile. She was ginger, like me. Except hers was more coppery, and in the summer it got lighter if she spent lots of time outside.*

*Some of the things I remember, I'm not sure if they're memories or if they're scenes from old home videos I've watched. They're fading now because the videos are gone, and I'm scared I won't always remember. I see them on a loop in my head most nights. Her holding me as I go down a slide, looking at animals at the zoo, playing hide-and-seek, eating ice cream and getting it on our noses, paddling in the sea.*

*She started getting sick when I was sev-en. I wanted to help look after her, but the sicker she got the more Dad kept me away from her. I was ten when she died, and I was there when it happened. She was my best friend. She was part of me and then she was gone, and I just didn't know how to get it to stop hurting so much. I wanted to talk to Dad about it, but he drank instead of talking.*

*I miss her. All the time. And I'm scared that she'd be disappointed in me.*

# FEBRUARY

FEBRUARY

# 55
## VIOLET

Freddie's nightmares were getting worse. They were happening almost every night, and Violet had started wedging a chair under her door and sleeping beside him with the hatch open so she could wake him before his thrashing escalated too much. Most of the time, his words were unintelligible, just mumblings and groanings, but last night Freddie had said one thing very clearly: Amy.

In the morning, when Violet asked him about it, his face lost all its color and she was sure his hands had started shaking, but he said, "No one, I don't know anyone called Amy." So, she told him to have a good day and left for school.

On the bus, tracing the raindrops as they skittered down the outside of the window, Violet leaned her forehead against the cool damp glass and sighed. Freddie was still writing in the notebook. He'd written so much about his mum that Violet felt as though she knew her. He'd written about his dad's drinking and how awful his stepmother had been. He'd written about his nights wandering town because he had nowhere to sleep and moving was better than staying still. He'd written about the youth shelter closing and how much worse things got after that because he simply wasn't cut out for the adult shelter, so he'd avoided it even when there were beds available. But there was a gap: the five years between Freddie's dad remarrying and Freddie ending up on the street were blank. A black hole in the timeline of Freddie. Something had happened. Something big. Violet was sure of it. And now, she was also sure that it had something to do with "Amy".

Part of her felt that maybe all Freddie needed was more time. But a bigger part, the part that heard him crying in his sleep and sat beside him when he woke up drenched in cold sweat, knew that Freddie wasn't dealing with it. He didn't have a therapist or friends or a family. All he had was Violet and her attic, and he had helped her so much that it just didn't seem fair.

So, Violet decided to meddle. She did what she'd promised herself she would never do: she scoured the internet for Freddie's name. Angling her phone toward the window as if someone might be prying over her shoulder, she tried every social media site she could think of but found nothing. Then she remembered his driving license: 12 All Saints Road, Olton. Maybe if she went there and spoke to Freddie's dad, she could build some bridges. It was a long shot, but it couldn't exactly make things any worse could it? And if it didn't work,

Freddie never needed to know.

Instead of disembarking opposite the school, Violet stayed on, waved sorry to Jeanette from the window, and texted her to say she'd explain tomorrow. Then she opened up Google Maps and typed in the address. The public transport symbol brought up three different routes, but the quickest told her that the ten-thirty bus from town, followed by a fifteen-minute walk, would take her to Freddie's old house.

\* \* \*

Three hours later, instead of being in math with Jeanette, Violet found herself standing opposite a large, red-brick house on a leafy street not too dissimilar from Walnut Avenue. It had a sloping driveway, a garage with a white door, and a large weeping willow in the front garden. She ascended the slope and tapped on the door. No answer. She rang the bell. Still nothing. They were probably at work.

She walked back to the pavement, sighed, and was about to start checking for bus times back home when someone from across the street called, "Everything okay, dear?" in a shaky old-person voice. Violet looked up and saw a gray-haired man leaning on a walking stick. She crossed the road.

"I'm looking for the Millers. Do they still live here?"

The man's smile wavered. "They left a few years ago, I'm afraid."

A few years? "Oh. It's just, my friend Freddie—Freddie Miller—has lost touch with his dad and he's trying to track him down."

282                       Cara Thurlbourn

"Freddie?" The man wasn't smiling, he looked...sad. "Poor boy. How is he?"

"He's good. He's doing good, but he's really desperate to find his dad."

"Well, after everything that happened, when they lost the house, the council relocated them. My wife might remember where they went. She was very fond of them, and I believe she tried to stay in touch with Janet."

"Would you mind asking her? It would be a huge help."

"Of course. Wait there, dear, might be a few minutes; I'm not as quick as I used to be."

The man trudged slowly back into his house, and fifteen minutes later returned with a piece of paper. "Rose says they lost the council place too. I hadn't realized. She hasn't heard from Janet in a while, but they did write each other a few times. Last Rose heard, they were living with Janet's mother on the outskirts of Newton. This is the address." The man paused and looked over at Freddie's old house. "Such a tragedy. Poor boy. Do give him my regards. He was always so polite."

Violet put the piece of paper into her pocket and said, "Thank you." She was about to turn away, when she added, "Sir, I'm sorry to ask, but would you mind telling me why they moved? You said something was a tragedy?"

The man's face hardened, and he tutted. "Oh no, I couldn't say. Not my place." Then he turned and walked, much more quickly, back inside.

# 56
## FREDDIE

Freddie hadn't left the attic for nearly three whole weeks. He'd done as Violet suggested, though, and filled out some trade school forms. And when he'd told her about the apprenticeship that Frank from the market had offered him, she'd squealed and jumped up and down, telling him it was all falling into place.

Freddie knew he should've felt that way too; everything he wanted, everything he thought he needed in order to get his life back on track, was starting to happen. Violet was his girlfriend, he had an offer of a job, and Violet had tracked down some social workers from the old youth shelter to be his references for trade school. He had saved enough money to secure a room to rent, just as soon as his apprenticeship was finalized, and Violet even said she was pretty sure that if they told her parents he'd been kicked out of his flat, they'd let him stay in her gran's old room until he'd sorted a new place. So, no more attic.

And yet, he didn't feel like it was falling into place. He felt the opposite: as if he were crumbling at the edges and there were too many pieces for him to try and hold on to. He'd been writing in the notebook Violet gave him. It helped, but there was so much he couldn't write. So much he was having to keep in. And the weight of it was so heavy that he could barely bring himself to climb down from the attic and shower before she returned home from school.

He was walking barefoot back from the bathroom with wet hair, and goose bumps on his arms, when the Johnsons' mail clattered through the mail slot. He hesitated. How long ago had he and Violet filled in the applications? Two weeks? They'd said they would write not email but, surely, it was too soon. He almost didn't go check, but then he told himself to at least look. And there it was: an envelope addressed to Mr. Frederick Miller.

Freddie carried his envelope to Violet's room and sat down on her bed. It was like lead in his hands, as if his entire future was waiting inside it. He put it down. Then he picked it up again, and gently, as if something might jump out at him, he peeled back the seal. There was just one sheet of paper inside. It was bound to be a no; a yes would be accompanied by paperwork. He lifted out the letter and unfolded it. He tried to scan it quickly, but his eyes couldn't read fast enough so he slowed down.

*Dear Mr. Miller . . . pleased to inform you . . . application accepted . . . . on the condition that you secure your own apprenticeship.*

He sprang up from the bed, holding the letter in both hands, reading it again. He'd been accepted. He kept reading: two days in school and three days as a *paid* apprentice. By next September, he'd be a qualified carpenter. If he worked hard, really hard, doing kitchens and doors and windows, one day he could buy a house, somewhere near a lake or a beach. He could make beautiful things out of driftwood—chairs and bookcases and ornaments—and Violet could draw. He was grinning so hard his cheeks ached. He had to tell Violet. He didn't care that she was at school. He had to tell her—now.

the Boy Who Lived in the Ceiling        285

# 57
## VIOLET

Freddie's stepmother's house wasn't far from Walnut Avenue, on a street called Granby Road. Violet hadn't ever been there, and the pin drop on the map on her phone wasn't very accurate because when she got to the spot where the house should've been there was nothing but commercial buildings: a small line of shops, a post office, and, next to them, a playground with swings and a big red slide.

She asked three people for directions. The first two shrugged, grumbled, and carried on walking. The third, an elderly lady who was resting on one of those walking sticks that turns into a stool, adjusted her glasses on the bridge of her nose, sucked in her cheeks, and said she thought it was the road behind the post office, but she couldn't be sure.

The estate behind the shops was new. The houses

stood proud and neat, squashed together with identical front doors, sparkling windows, and tiny gardens. The visitors' parking area was still fenced off, unfinished, at the end of the street so cars lined the road instead. Violet turned herself sideways and shimmied between a blue Renault Clio and a Fiesta the color of mustard. She checked the piece of paper Rose had given her: *Bell Cottage, Granby Road.* But there were no cottages here and no houses with names, just numbers. She was about to give up when she saw a narrow, graveled road with a sign that said *Granby Avenue*. She tucked the piece of paper back in her pocket and, clasping her phone as if she might need to suddenly call 9-9-9, she stepped onto the gravel.

Granby Avenue was boxed in by a tall stone wall on one side and a wooden fence on the other. Then, without warning, it disappeared, replaced by a patch of thinning grass and a huddle of spiky, dark-green trees. Violet stopped. Surely it didn't lead nowhere? She looked around, half expecting the cottage to materialize in front of her, like something from Harry Potter, but there was nothing but the gravely path and the distant hum of traffic. Maybe the cottage had been knocked down?

Violet walked over to the first of the spiky trees and brushed her palm against its fronds. She moved to the second tree and did the same, then the third, and then she realized that the trees weren't all part of the same huddle; there was a gap in the middle. A gap that was only just big enough to admit a car. Through the gap, slightly uphill on a mound of patchy grass, stood a short square cottage. Dark-brown tendrils of leafless ivy crawled up its face, and the roof was missing several slates. The curtains were drawn. It looked abandoned.

Violet moved closer and noticed a black metal bell hanging above the front door. Its tinny chime echoed as it caught in the breeze. Back through the gap, the crisp afternoon sun had warmed her face and hands, but here, behind the trees, it was like the cottage was wrapped in something cold and sad that made everything appear in black and white. This had to be it. There was nothing else here.

Before ringing the bell, Violet tugged her jacket a little tighter and put a loose strand of hair back behind her ear. She breathed in. The doorbell trilled in the hallway, slicing through the stillness. For a long time, there was no movement, and then the soft suck of air indicated that someone within had opened a door. A silhouette paused, then reached out an arm, slid across the bolt at the top of the doorframe, and turned a key in the lock. The woman who opened the door looked like she hadn't seen daylight for months. Her face was drawn, her skin stretched so tight across her cheekbones that Violet was afraid it would tear if she spoke.

The woman said nothing.

Violet shuffled her feet, then said, "Hello," trying to sound both confident and friendly. "Mrs. Miller?"

The woman nodded and glanced down, taking in Violet's velvet leggings and knee-high socks.

"I'm Violet Johnson. I'm a friend of Freddie's."

Mrs. Miller's eyes flickered briefly, but her face remained unchanged. She wrapped her cardigan tighter around her chest. "You'd better come in," she said. "Please take off your shoes."

Violet left her shoes next to the front door and followed Janet Miller down a dark hallway and into a dark kitchen. The blinds were drawn, but instead of opening them, Janet flicked on the lights. "Would you like a cup of tea?" she asked perfunctorily, not because she was being friendly but because this was what you did when you had visitors.

Violet said, "Yes, please," and Janet told her to take a seat.

Violet perched stiffly on one of the wooden chairs at the kitchen table, watching her host prepare the tea. The chair's legs were uneven, and every now and then, it toppled to the right and made an abrupt thudding sound. Violet thought that, probably, there was a time when Mrs. Miller would have been beautiful. Her hair was thick and dark, and her eyes were dazzlingly blue, but her frame was pinched and fragile, swamped by the bulky cardigan and a pair of loose-fitting jeans. Janet handed Violet a cup of pale tea and sat down opposite her with a glass of water.

"Oh, I'm sorry," Violet said, "you didn't want one?"

Janet looked confused.

"Tea?"

"I don't drink it," she replied.

Violet sipped the tea; a fuzzy, metallic taste coated her tongue, but she smiled and said thank you. Now that she was here, she didn't know what to say. Janet tapped her fingernails on her water glass.

"Is, um, Mr. Miller around?" Violet asked tentatively.

"No. My husband isn't here."

"Oh. I was hoping to talk to him about Freddie. Will he be back soon?"

Janet Miller straightened herself in her chair and released a slow, controlled breath. Her jaw twitched, and she placed her hands very deliberately, palms down, on the table as though she was steadying herself. "My husband is an alcoholic," she said, looking straight into Violet's eyes. "He's in rehab. I don't know when he will be home." The bluntness of the words made Violet flinch. Mrs. Miller blinked and sipped her water.

"I'm sorry," Violet said, because it felt like the right thing to say. "I just..." She paused; once she started there would be no going back. Janet raised her eyebrows. Violet continued. "It's Freddie," she said. "You see, I'm not sure if you know, but he doesn't have anywhere to live."

Janet didn't flinch.

"He's homeless," Violet added, trying to make it sink in. "He's literally been sleeping on the streets. For nearly two years and, from what I can work out, he thinks that you hate him. But I told him that simply can't be true. You're his family. Families forgive each other, right? And whatever happened between you, I just know you wouldn't want him living like that. He's in a really bad way, and I just think that—"

Janet held up her hand as if she was a traffic warden stopping a line of cars. "Let me stop you there," she said tightly. "Freddie is not my family."

Violet opened her mouth and closed it again.

"Freddie is Robert's son. Not mine." Janet stood up, her face flushed pink and her words were tumbling over one another in their urgency. "Freddie ruined this family. He took everything from us. We had nothing. The only reason we're here in this godforsaken, soul-sucking house and have been able to get Robert the help he

needs is because my witch of a mother died. If it hadn't
been for her, *we* would have been on the street. Robert
would have pickled his liver and be dead in the gutter,
and God knows where I'd be. But she died, and we're
here. Despite everything, we're here and Robert is getting better and we're trying to rebuild our lives." Janet
was gesticulating wildly now, her jagged collar bones
moving up and down as she flung out her arms. "So,
whatever you have to say about Freddie, I don't want
to hear it. He has no family; he deserves no family. He
deserves *nothing*." The venom with which she spat her
last words seemed to drain the last of her energy, and
she reached out a hand to steady herself.

Violet hung her head. "I'm sorry," she muttered. "I
shouldn't have come."

"No, you shouldn't."

There was nothing else to say. Janet gathered the
glass of water and the remains of Violet's insipid tea and
tipped them into the sink, turning her back and hunching
over the washing-up bowl, her shoulders trembling.

Violet walked softly down the hallway and picked up
her shoes. She bent down to tie her laces, and when
she looked up, she noticed a cluster of picture frames
on the wall. All of them were empty. Still hanging there,
but empty. All except one: a photograph of Janet Miller
and a man who looked like an older, grayer version of
Freddie. Janet and Freddie's dad were sitting on a picnic
blanket, smiling. And between them sat a little girl. A girl
with a swirly silver necklace that said *Amy*.

# 58

## FREDDIE

Violet wasn't at school. Freddie waited and waited by the gates, but she didn't come out, so when he saw a girl he recognized from Violet's phone, he waved and said, "Hiya, sorry, are you Violet's friend?"

The girl scowled at him. She had a moon-shaped face and small eyes. "Yeah."

"I'm her boyfriend. Was she in today? I need to talk to her." He was speaking quickly, the electrifying sensation of actually having some energy was tingling in his arms and his legs.

"No. She stayed on the bus. She texted and said she'd explain tomorrow."

"Oh." Freddie frowned. "Okay, thanks. Never mind."

As he walked away from the school, he glanced at his watch. He had time. So, he jumped on the next bus that came along and headed straight for the supermarket.

* * *

An hour later, Freddie boarded the bus back to Walnut Avenue, clutching his acceptance letter, a bunch of sunflowers, and a bottle of pink bubbly stuff that wasn't champagne but looked like it.

Violet was going to be so proud of him.

Violet's fingers were shaking. She trusted Freddie, didn't she? After everything, hadn't he proved to her that he was a good, kind person? It didn't matter what had happened in his past. It had never mattered. Except, now, it did.

It was Janet. Something about Janet Miller's face and the seething hatred in her eyes had made Violet look at Freddie differently. It had made her question everything because, really, she knew nothing about him. Only what he'd written in their notebook, and he could have made that up. He could have been anyone. He could have done anything.

She looked up, as if Freddie might've been able to hear her treacherous thoughts through the ceiling. But she couldn't stop herself. The question echoed around her brain, bouncing between her ears, giving her a headache. *What had Freddie done? What had Freddie done? What had Freddie done?*

Eventually, she took a deep breath and opened her laptop. Into the search box, she typed,

*Amy Miller. Mother Janet. Brother Freddie. Olton.*

The results flashed up almost instantaneously. And Violet felt her fingers grip the edge of her laptop.

**OLTON HERALD: Girl, five, killed by own brother.**

**NORFOLK STAR: Tragic accident. Five-year-old girl dead.**

**DAILY POST: Girl dead in tragic accident. Brother guilty.**

Violet felt her stomach lurch and ran to the bathroom. She vomited hard into the toilet, with no time to even lift the seat up or hold her hair back. When she'd finished, she sat back on the cold, tiled floor and wiped her mouth with the back of her hand. Beads of sweat had formed at the base of her neck. The words *Freddie killed Amy* were swimming in front of her eyes. She took off her glasses and pinched the bridge of her nose. She told herself to calm down. Accident, the headlines had said. An accident.

Walking back to her room with shaky legs and clammy hands, Violet saw Scruff hurtle through her door. He made a playful groaning sound. The door to her courtyard clicked. Shit. Freddie.

Violet was too late. When she entered the bedroom, Freddie was kneeling at the side of her bed, peering at her laptop. One hand hovered above the mousepad, the other was clutching a bottle of wine. When he saw her, he stumbled to his feet and lost his grip on the bottle. It bounced on the carpet but didn't break.

"You googled me?" he asked. A ridiculous phrase; usually it made Violet giggle because it sounded rude. But the hurt Freddie's voice cut her in two, and googling wasn't even a little bit funny anymore. Every single one of his features seemed to have folded in on itself, as if his bones had turned to jelly. He leaned sideways and his shoulder butted up against the wall. If it hadn't been there, he might have fallen over.

"Freddie. I..." Violet's eyes jolted wildly from Freddie to the laptop. She had no excuse and, before she could stop herself, it all came tumbling out. "I tracked down your stepmother. I went to see her. I thought I could help. She said...she said some awful things, and I didn't know what to think. I'm sorry."

She expected him to be angry. Perhaps that's what happened to Amy. A tragic accident—he'd had a temper, he'd pushed her, she'd fallen. "Freddie..."

He jumped back like a caged animal anticipating a whip. And then he was gone. He simply turned, flew back through the door, over the courtyard wall. Gone. And Violet was left with her laptop and Google and an empty space.

\* \* \*

She was still staring at the spot where Freddie should have stood, when a tiny voice behind her said, "Vi? Freddie here?"

Violet turned slowly to face her little brother. She

felt suddenly, overwhelmingly, protective of him and wrapped her arms tightly around his miniature frame. She squeezed, and Jamie giggled, pushing her off, then shouting, "Scruff!" and charging back into the hallway. Violet's stomach tugged downward, and she reached for her phone. She scrolled through her photos to the one of Freddie, Jamie, and Scruff. She didn't know what to do. Should she read the articles? Chase after Freddie? Where would he even go?

She sat down and turned her laptop back toward her. There was no point avoiding it now. She might as well find out. She clicked the second search result. A picture of Freddie—younger, clean shaven, fuller in the face, and smiling broadly—and then the article:

**Tragic accident. Five-year-old girl dead.**

A family from Olton are in mourning after their five-year-old daughter, Amy, was tragically killed. Amy Miller ran outside to say goodbye to her brother Frederick Miller, 17, but he accidentally reversed into her in the family car. She was pronounced dead at the scene. A close friend said, "It was absolutely horrific. The poor family. Can you imagine how they're feeling? Freddie had only just gotten his license. He's such a lovely boy. How will he live with himself after this? It's unthinkable." So far, the family have declined to comment.

# 60
## FREDDIE

He had nowhere to go. There wasn't a single place on Earth that would allow him to escape from himself. So, he went to see Amy.

# MARCH

MARCH

# 61

## VIOLET

Freddie had been gone for over a week. Her mum and dad thought they'd broken up because she'd barely stopped crying and had turned the feather he'd carved her into a necklace that she hadn't taken off. On the third day, she'd ventured up into the attic and emptied the contents of his backpack onto his sleeping bag. Inside a tattered children's book, she'd found a single photograph of Amy and Freddie wearing party hats and face paints. Freddie was a tiger. Amy was a dog.

After that, she couldn't wait any longer. She couldn't just sit and wait and hope he came back. She tried the Kitchen, but Gina said she hadn't seen him and looked at Violet like she wanted to kill her. She tried the church and left her number with the vicar in case Freddie showed up. She walked up and down the main street, peering into coffee shop windows. But there was no sign of him. Freddie had vanished.

There was only one thing left to try.

* * *

The bus seemed to take longer than it had last time, just
to spite her. By the time she reached Freddie's old house,
it was late afternoon. The man she'd spoken to before
wasn't home, but his wife, Rose, scribbled the address
down on a piece of paper from a little blue notepad next
to the hall telephone. "There, dear, that's the cemetery.
It's not far." Violet thanked her and adjusted her bag on
her shoulder. It was heavy, but she probably deserved
the discomfort.

Amy's headstone was in a sheltered spot beneath a
tree that left dappled spots of sunlight across its brow,
like the fairy lights in Freddie's attic. In between two baby
cherubs, there was a black and white photograph of her.

*Amy Catherine Miller*
*Beloved Daughter to Robert and Janet*
*2012–2017*

Violet wrapped her arms around herself and closed
her eyes. Freddie wasn't even mentioned. His role as
Amy's brother had been erased from history. Bending
down, she opened her bag and removed the large hardcover volume inside it. She placed the book gently in
front of Amy's grave, blew a kiss, and left.

# 62

## FREDDIE

Freddie slept by Amy's grave for six entire nights. No one disturbed him. No one asked him to leave. Then, on the seventh night, it rained—the kind of rain that hurts your face, pummels the pavements, and knocks leaves from trees. In the morning, the small stuffed unicorn that he'd brought and positioned beside a jar of daisies was absolutely sodden. Amy would have hated it. She would have begged him to make the unicorn better, dry it out, fluff it up. So, he went to buy another one. After that, he had just ten pounds left in his pocket and this would be the last of it, but he didn't care, so he also bought a small see-through plastic shoebox to put it in and, as he tucked it inside, whispered, "This will keep you safe."

It was twilight when he arrived back at the cemetery. As he had in the days before Violet, he'd walked from the town center, so he had less time being still and alone with his thoughts. Approaching Amy's grave, his stomach tightened. Someone had left something on it. He was getting ready to grab whatever it was, tear it to pieces, and roar at the sky, when he stopped. It was a book. A book he knew by heart. He bobbed down and picked it up, placing the boxed pink unicorn in its place. *Hope is the Thing with Feathers—The Complete Poems of Emily Dickinson*. The very same edition Violet had first given him. He opened it. Inside, there was an inscription:

*Darling Freddie,*
*Come home, and we'll make it right. It wasn't your fault.*
*Yours, always and always, Violet*

Freddie stared at the words.

*It wasn't your fault.*

No one had said that to him before. Not the police, not his friends, no one.

At the hospital, he'd been in shock. Unable to speak or move. There had been lights and noise and too many people, and none of them had been telling him what was happening. He'd been made to wait in the hallway with a policewoman who was trying not to cry. He'd kept expecting his dad or Janet to burst through the double doors, smiling, saying everything was all right, but they hadn't. Freddie had waited for hours until, eventually, a doctor with an eerily still face had bobbed down in front of him and told him that Amy was dead.

He'd wanted to see her. He'd wanted to say sorry and bury his head on her tiny little shoulder, but they wouldn't let him.

The policewoman had taken Freddie home and, nearly twelve hours later, his dad and Janet had returned. They hadn't shouted or cried or told him to leave. They'd just walked right past him as if he hadn't been there. Janet had gone to Amy's room and closed the door. His father had gone to the kitchen and opened a bottle of whiskey.

And each day had continued just like that—right up to the funeral and beyond. Freddie had longed for his dad to speak to him, even if it was to tell him he hated him. He'd longed for Janet to look at him and make a snide comment about his untidy hair or lack of discipline. But they hadn't, and it was as if he'd died too.

He thought it was the Johnsons' attic that had turned him into some kind of ghost but, really, he was a phantom long before that. And suddenly, staring at Violet's note, Freddie realized he was ready to be seen again.

# JULY

JUL

# 63
## VIOLET

It was nearly summer vacation. Violet had survived the tail end of the academic year, but now she was ready for a break. She and Jeanette were planning a camping trip. Camping wasn't really Violet's thing, but Jeanette had won her over with wide-eyed talk of campfires and marshmallows and starry skies, and now, Violet was almost looking forward to it.

Sitting on her bed, she opened a small wooden box and stroked the note that was taped to the inside of its lid.

*Thank you for everything. I'm the only one who can make this right. I love you. Freddie x*

She'd come home, just a few days after leaving the book beside Amy's grave, to find the box and the note in her courtyard. Inside, she'd put the feather Freddie had carved for her, the postcards they'd swapped, the photos she'd printed from her phone...

Someone tapped on her door.

She closed the box with a snap and shoved it back under her bed. "Yep, come in."

As she looked up, Jeanette burst into the room, waving her arms. She was gasping for breath, her cheeks were beet red, and the buttons of her blouse were straining as her chest heaved up and down.

"I...I..."

Violet shepherded her onto the bed. "What on earth's happened?"

Jeanette sucked in a big deep breath. "Give me your laptop..."

Violet handed it over. "Jeanette—"

"So you know that awesome documentary maker I follow? The one from around here? Grahaeme Gallows?"

"Um..."

Jeanette rolled her eyes as if Violet should've remembered this information. "He mainly does serious stuff? But he's *so* into musical theatre too. He's like the first person really to be super cool and champion both and talk about how musicals are some of the most—"

"Jeanette..." Violet was becoming impatient.

"Well. Okay, just look..."

Jeanette turned the screen so that Violet could see it and pressed play on a YouTube video. One second it was black, and then staring back at her...

*"Hi. My name's Freddie. Frederick Miller. And I'm homeless..."*

Violet slid down to the floor, leaning up against the bed, taking the laptop with her.

*"I didn't think I wanted anyone to know my story, but the thing is, if no one knows, then nothing will ever change. So, here I am."*

Violet and Jeanette watched as Freddie, followed by a jerky handheld camera, walked down Newton High Street. He was wearing clothes she hadn't seen before—old clothes, too-big clothes, dirty clothes—and carrying a crumpled backpack.

The camera followed him as he sat down in a doorway near Starbucks, took a baseball cap from his bag, and placed it on his lap.

Violet shuddered but made herself keep watching.

There was a voiceover now—Grahaeme Gallows talking about homeless people feeling invisible. The camera focused on the faces of the people walking past, caught them looking away, zoomed in on Freddie's empty hat. And then it cut to Freddie in a public bathroom, taking off his clothes.

Violet frowned and looked at Jeanette.

"Keep watching, Vi," she said.

So, Violet did.

She watched as Freddie changed into a suit and returned to Starbucks. She watched as he smiled charmingly, approached person after person with stories of losing his wallet, being in trouble with his boss, misplacing a company credit card. She watched as these people looked him in the eye, laughed with him, touched him lightly on the shoulder...and gave him money. She watched as Freddie told the world his deepest secrets.

He told them about his mum dying and his dad's drinking. He told them that he used to be a straight-A student, popular, confident, and happy—despite what was going on at home.

And then he told them about Amy.

He scraped his fingers through his hair and choked back tears as he told them that he'd run out of the house one day when his dad and his step-mum had been arguing. That he hadn't been looking when he'd put the car into reverse. That he hadn't realized Amy had followed him.

"I'd turned up my music. I don't remember what it was, but it was loud. I didn't see her. I thought I was in first gear, but I was in reverse. And there was this...bump."

Violet shuddered. Jeanette reached for her hand.

On-screen, Freddie was trembling. "I thought she'd be okay. I didn't realize she'd...I didn't know she was dead. I thought she'd be okay."

Violet wanted so badly to wrap her arms around him. She wanted to stroke his hair and tell him it wasn't his fault—to say out loud the words she'd written to him.

Freddie wiped his eyes with his sleeve and breathed in sharply. "After Amy, everything fell apart. Dad's drinking got worse. We lost the house and moved into a housing association place, but then we lost that too, and I ended up with nowhere to go."

\* \* \*

The film was an hour long, and Violet watched it from beginning to end, twice.

The Director—Grahaeme—spoke to homeless teen-agers, the staff from the closed-down youth shelter, girls younger than Violet who were couch-surfing because they had nowhere else to stay...so many people. But the last frame was Freddie, looking straight into the camera.

*"For such a long time, I thought I wasn't worth saving. But then I met someone who changed my life. She made me see that there is still light in the dark. There's still good. There's still hope. And I hope that one day she can forgive me because, finally, I think I'm learning to forgive myself."*

# OCTOBER

OCTOBER

# 69
## FREDDIE & VIOLET

VIOLET: ETA?

FREDDIE: Just finishing kitchen job at No.5. Probably 7:30.

VIOLET: Mum says r u staying over?

FREDDIE: Depends. Is ur dad making breakfast tomorrow?

VIOLET: He says if u let him beat u at cards then yeah :-D

FREDDIE: Spare room?

VIOLET: Depends.

FREDDIE: On?

VIOLET: Whether I like u enough to sneak u into mine.

FREDDIE: I think u do.

VIOLET: Maybe.

FREDDIE: On bus. See u soon.

VIOLET: Love u.

FREDDIE: Love u too (more than donuts).

VIOLET: !!!

# A LOOK AT: THE GIRL WHO WASN'T (AN ARHURST NOVEL)

**A touching coming-of-age story about how far we're willing to go to find a lasting friendship.**

Jeanette's life currently revolves around caring for her agoraphobic and hoarder mother, all while dreaming of attending university for a musical theater course. When her mother's illness worsens, she finds solace in a new friendship, but there's one problem: the friendship started with a lie after she created a fake profile under the name of Marcia.

Jack seems to have it all together, but his home life is anything but perfect. His mother is violent towards his father and, because of her own career as a professional tennis player, she doesn't want Jack to pursue his love of music, but instead, college football. Jack's one comfort is Marica, but when he finds out the truth, he is not sure what or who to believe.

Attempting to escape their own problems, Jeanette and Jack lean on a new-found friendship and learn that not everyone is who they seem to be.

*AVAILABLE SEPTEMBER 2021*

# ABOUT THE AUTHOR

Cara Thurlbourn is a UK writer with a passion for all kinds of storytelling, particularly Young Adult books. She studied English at the University of Nottingham and for an MA in Publishing Studies in Oxford before embarking on a career in the industry. Cara worked as an editor for nearly ten years but in 2016, the year she turned 30, she turned her hand to writing and has never looked back.

Cara currently lives in a small, picturesque village in the Suffolk countryside with Mr. T and Mini T.

CPSIA information can be obtained
at www.ICGtesting.com
Printed in the USA
LVHW041926041121
702459LV00014B/615

9 781953 944085